There Better Be Pie

―――

Jessica Gadziala

Copyright © 2019 Jessica Gadziala
All rights reserved. In accordance with the U.S Copyright Act of 1976, the scanning, uploading, and electronic sharing of any part of this book without permission of the publisher is unlawful piracy and theft of the author's intellectual property. This book or any portion thereof may not be reproduced or used in any manner whatsoever without the express written permission of the author except for brief quotations used in a book review.

"This book is a work of fiction. The names, characters, places and incidents are products of the writer's imagination or have been used fictitiously and are not to be construed as real. Any resemblance to persons, living or dead, actual events, locales or organizations is entirely coincidental."

Cover image credit: Shutterstock .com/Oksana Mizina

CHAPTER ONE

Juliette

Who would have thought one simple sentence could ruin my absolute favorite holiday?

Trip is coming to spend the weekend with us.

Just like that, all my hopes of a relaxing time with my parents up at their house in Maine, spending time cuddled up watching movies, drinking spiked cider and hot toddies, and eating until we had to change into more forgiving pants, were dashed.

I mean, if there was a single person I was least likely to cuddle up next to watching movies, or stuff my face in front of, it was Trip Martin.

Though, with his presence there, I would definitely still be drinking spiked cider and hot toddies. Likely in much larger quantities.

"Stop grinding your teeth," my mother demanded over the phone, as she had needed to do countless times over the years.

Everyone had their nervous habits. My father paced. My mother cleaned. And I ground my teeth. Much to the chagrin of my dentist. And my mother since the sound 'went right through' her skull.

THERE BETTER BE PIE

"You can't just drop a bomb like that on me and expect me to take it with a smile," I reminded her.

"Oh, honey. Trip is a nice man. I don't know why the two of you have decided to hate each other so much."

There was a long, long list of reasons why I personally hated Trip Martin.

The list for why he hated me seemed to consist of two things, though.

One—I was born wealthy.

Two—I didn't work at the family business.

That was it.

At least that was all I could tell from all our interactions over the years.

Trip was a blue-collar guy through-and-through. And he couldn't imagine anyone wanting to work anywhere but at my family's three generations old luxury car business.

Yes, as in those custom cars you saw billionaires and celebrities driving around that cost more than the average middle-class family would see in their lifetime.

My great grandfather had come into some money from his father, which he had used to start production on the first Kensley car—the epitome of luxury in every way. He had lucked out in that the car came out around the time when the country was starting to see its first real boom in millionaires.

As a family, we were all incredibly fortunate in that the world just kept creating more millionaires and billionaires as time went on—the kind of people who wanted exclusivity and an anal attention to every small detail like our Kensley Automobiles provided.

It was a thriving business that turned an insane profit for my family. The kind of profit that allowed my parents to own an estate in Maine that we only went to for Thanksgiving. Yet kept staffed year-round.

So Trip was right about that. I was born wealthy. But that was also not my fault nor my choosing. It was just how things were. I really couldn't imagine why he would use it as a reason to have a personal grudge against me.

THERE BETTER BE PIE

As for not working at the family business. Well, he was right about that as well. The only thing was, he didn't understand why; he didn't know the history behind that decision. Since he was a pompous ass, I didn't ever feel the need to explain myself to him either.

I just avoided him.

Whenever possible.

Of course, there were always times when it was unavoidable. My father had a thriving business, but he also had a very tight-knit community of workers. He wanted everyone to feel like they were part of a big family. As such, there were holiday parties and summer retreats that he arranged and paid for. Things he expected my mother and I to attend as well. Since we were part of his big family and he didn't want it to seem like he was drawing a line between his real family and his work family.

So Trip and I—unfortunately—bumped into each other at least three times a year. Every year since he started working at Kensley years before.

Luckily, there was enough of a buffer of time in between each meeting that I cooled down enough from whatever heated argument we had gotten into that I didn't want to immediately rip out his vocal cords the next time we ran into each other.

Time had the ability to blur the edges of memories, soften the hard feelings.

The problem was, I had just seen him at the masked gala my parents had hosted at their home for Kensley employees and their families.

Twenty-something days was not nearly enough time to forget how much pleasure I might derive in seeing the man with the runaway mouth suddenly being struck mute.

"He's a tool. And he thinks I'm a spoiled brat."

"He does not think that."

My mother was a saint. An actual living saint who never thought a bad thing about anyone. I was sure the woman could find something nice to say about every

THERE BETTER BE PIE

murderer currently locked behind bars, no matter how heinous their crimes may be.

Why I didn't seem to inherit that ability to think and say only pleasant things about others was beyond me. I guess I got a little more of my father's temper, the passionate way he always defended his beliefs and actions.

"He calls me Princess, Mom."

"Oh, but that is sweet! What girl doesn't want to be called a princess?"

He didn't call me a princess because he thought I was rare and beautiful and spectacular.

He spat it at me like an insult.

Spoiled little princess was the inflection.

"Is he just coming for Thanksgiving dinner?" I asked, knowing it was pointless to try to convince her that we genuinely just didn't like each other.

"He is coming up Wednesday afternoon with your father. And leaving with him Tuesday morning."

Oh, good God.

Was there no mercy in the universe?

Granted, it was a large house with plenty of room so that we wouldn't literally be rubbing shoulders when we tried to move past each other. Still, it wasn't so big that I could avoid him entirely. At least not without offending my mother who worked her butt off to make Thanksgiving something to be remembered.

She was already up at the Maine house, taking charge of the decorating, making sure the rooms were cleaned up to par, creating grocery lists, helping the staff with the shopping.

The staff would all be heading out on Wednesday morning, not to show up again until we were all on our way home.

My mom and I would be in charge of all the cooking and baking and cleaning up after the actual meals.

It was something she loved.

It was usually something I enjoyed as well. There was nothing that brought the memories of my childhood

THERE BETTER BE PIE

back quite like being at her side, using special cutters and stamps to make shapes to use as pie crust tops. There was no simple latticework on her pies, oh no. Each and every one was a masterpiece, almost too pretty to eat. Though eat them we did. I, especially, did.

It was the one time of year where I allowed myself to pig out entirely. Without shame. Without worrying about my waistline.

And now I would have to do that in front of someone I loathed entirely?

Ugh.

"I think you two will learn to understand each other a lot more by spending some time around each other," my mom insisted.

"Maybe you're right." And maybe I would want to see him driven through with a spike, ala Vlad-The-Impaler style.

"You'll see, darling. It is all going to work out."

"You always put on the best Thanksgiving," I told her, wanting to get away from the topic of Trip, feeling like my blood pressure was rising just from a simple phone conversation about the man.

"Remember to pack warm, Jett. It is colder than New York."

The house was lovely, but old, drafty, warmed mostly by fireplaces because it would be too expensive to try to keep the heat in if you used the actual heating system.

That meant that you left smelling the smoke in your hair and clothes, something that always made me a little sad as I drove all the way back down to my New York City apartment, wanting to turn right around and go back.

It was pointless, though.

My family would be already on their way back to their place in Pennsylvania. They didn't need to live so close to the plant. My father didn't need to go into work every day. But he loved it. And my mother adored their ancient Victorian. They'd bought when it had been nothing but rotting wood, wiring problems, and leaks coming through the roof in every room, then painstakingly went about restoring it to its previous glory. It was the most beautiful place in the world, and I totally understood my mother's love of it.

I hoped, one day, to be able to get a fixer-upper of my own, something that I saw the potential in even if nobody else did, then show the world how wrong they were about it.

That house would likely be somewhere close to theirs as well.

I lived in the 'big city'—as my mother put it—but I was a small-town girl at heart. I liked knowing my neighbors and catching up while bumping into one another in the local bakery or convenience store.

The city had its perks. Namely, job opportunities. And, let's face it, not enough could be said for takeaway that would be delivered to your door at three a.m. when you had a craving.

It was my temporary home.

I hadn't even bothered to unpack the antique China set I'd inherited from my grandmother, choosing to keep it tucked away in the back of my closet. It took up precious shoe real estate, sure, but it somehow felt wrong to put that set in the cupboards of a home that didn't really feel like home to me.

But, for now, it would have to do.

I figured I had another five years at my job. After that, the plan was my forever place, my forever town, the life I had been working toward since I moved to the city.

Until then, I made do with that 'home' feeling whenever I spent the holidays with my parents.

Which was why I was so frustrated by the presence of an interloper.

Especially the Devil himself.

"Will do. Do you need me to bring anything up?"

"You always find the best beer for your father. Oh, but buy double this time. I believe Trip is a beer drinker too."

THERE BETTER BE PIE

Oh, I would get him beer alright.

Because my mother asked it of me.

But that wouldn't stop me from secretly hoping he might choke on it.

"Sounds like a plan. If you think of anything else, let me know. I have a couple stops on the way up, so I can get any last-minute things you forgot."

"I will keep that in mind. See you in a few days, honey. Love you."

"Love you too."

I did, too. Which was why I was going to try really, really hard not to get riled by Trip. Even if he provoked it. Which he almost always did. I would just need to work harder to keep my cool.

For my father's sake. Since Trip was the son he'd never had.

And for my mother's sake because I knew she would wring her hands and worry herself sick about it.

She hated conflict of any sort. She'd never once even grounded me because she didn't like the look of anger or disappointment she'd anticipated I would have.

Soft hearts like hers were precious and rare. I did everything in my power not to make her worry too much, to get upset.

This, though; this would be the hardest thing I had ever done, since there had yet to be a situation in which Trip and I didn't end up nearly screaming at each other. I swear I nearly hauled off and hit him once for snarking at me at our annual Easter egg event.

If there hadn't been so many kids around, I might have actually done it. And I had never hit someone before in my life.

That was just the effect Trip Martin had on me.

It was going to be a long, long holiday.

After a long, long drive.

Eight and a half hours if I didn't hit traffic. But, let's face it, I was going to hit traffic. I would be lucky if I made it in ten.

THERE BETTER BE PIE

This meant that if I wanted to make it there before my father and Trip did, I would need to leave sometime around four in the morning.

Sighing, I climbed off the off-white tufted couch that looked as beautiful in person as it had in the catalog—with absolutely no comfort whatsoever—and made my way to my shoebox of a bedroom, hauling my luggage out from under my bed. All four of them.

I was not, by any stretch of the word, a light packer. I had this almost compulsive need to be prepared for any possible situation.

There was a hot tub on the deck. Despite never having gone in it in the ten years since they'd bought the Maine estate, I needed to pack a bathing suit just in case. Getting hot tub drunk suddenly sounded like a very viable way to spend some time when Trip and I couldn't seem to play nice.

Then, of course, there were the usual outfits. Bedtime, normal, with some extras in case of rain or snow, then something fancy for Thanksgiving dinner itself since we liked to keep that tradition even though it—usually—was just family for the holiday. Then, since it was cold, there needed to be a sweater or two, a hat, scarf, gloves, slippers, and a heavy robe.

And then, well, then there were shoes.

I had a whole suitcase just for the shoes.

It was overkill, I knew, but the whole point of buying nice shoes was to be able to wear them whenever possible. I could sometimes be found walking around in my apartment on a Sunday morning in a pair of panties, a plain white tee, and a pair of Louboutins my mother had gotten me for my last birthday.

Shoes had been one of those things for me. That comfort item. The thing that always made me feel great even if I felt bad about myself in every other way. It was an obsession I had developed in high school when I was cripplingly insecure about clothes, about trying to hide this or that. I hadn't been a thin girl. In fact, my mother had

THERE BETTER BE PIE

always lovingly referred to me as her Little Pudge Muffin up until I finally lost a bit of the weight in college. Not all of it. I still was a tad curvier than was ever in vogue, but I no longer got lectured by doctors or felt weird buying a bathing suit. But all through those insecure years, shoes had been there for me, had been a focal point that I felt drew people's attention away from my body and onto my feet.

As a much more secure adult, though, they never lost their appeal. They still were the impulse buy when I'd had a bad day. They were still what I planned entire outfits around.

I indulged myself because it was my one real vice. And as far as vices go, this one was tame. A little taxing on my pocketbook, sure, but relatively healthy otherwise.

So I went ahead and threw in knee-high snow boots with faux fur trim, booties, boots, and three pairs of stilettos.

Practical? Nope.

But also somehow completely necessary in my mind.

Finished, I zipped everything up, placing it all beside my door to taunt me for the next few days as I went about my daily life.

Eventually, the pile got a couple bottles of wine, six-packs of craft beers, and—lastly—a gorgeous bouquet of lilies my mother would insist was unnecessary, but would fawn over the entire long weekend.

The morning of, I got up at three a.m., put the bare minimum of effort into my appearance, grabbed two coffees—one for each cup holder—loaded down my trunk, and hit the road hours before sun up.

I'd like to say I did this with an upbeat attitude, that I had talked myself into being cheerful, that I was only expecting positive things.

But the fact of the matter was, I was crabby and tired and ready for a fight.

The world around me seemed to be in agreement with my mood, the sky pouring down rain in angry bursts through several states, deadlocking traffic, leaving me soaked through to my underwear after having to get out to get gas and refills on my coffee.

I was wet, shivering, and in desperate need of my mother's warm welcome when I finally pulled up to the house.

But it wasn't my mother who was there to greet me.
Oh, no.
That was freaking Trip Martin.

CHAPTER TWO

Juliette

Of course it was him.
Standing there on the front porch with that stern brow that always seemed to be directed at me, annoyed and disappointed.
As if he had any right to have expectations of me in general.
"Keep it together," I whispered to myself, taking a deep breath, chugging the last dregs of cold coffee, then slinging some still-wet dark hair out of my face.
I suddenly wished I had pulled off on a side street, taken a minute to try to get myself back together. One glance in the rearview let me know that my eyelids were puffy from eye strain, the purple smudges underneath making the honey-colored eyes that I generally considered my best feature look drab and lifeless.
A little concealer and mascara would have gone a long way to making me look less like a swamp creature.
Though why I was worried about how I looked around someone I disliked so entirely was beyond me.
I guess it went back to that dread we all hold in our hearts about running into that Mean Girl from high school

on the *one* day when we left the house in sweats with our hair in a messy bun and a completely naked face.

We always wanted to look our best around the people we liked the least. It was a self-preservation thing.

It was too late now, though, to whip out my emergency touch-up bag and make myself feel a bit better.

Of course, the situation was only exacerbated by the fact that guys like Trip Martin simply looked stupidly flawless at all times with absolutely no effort. And I meant none. He seemed to only bother to shave once every week or two. His dirty blond was always at an economical length; he never seemed to actually need to style it to make it look charmingly disheveled. Then he went ahead and had a jaw that could cut glass, eyes the most striking shade of sky blue framed in medium brown lashes that made me wonder why in the world men always ended up with the lashes we had to glue on.

No one would ever accuse Trip of being particularly fashionable. While he no longer worked on the production line, getting his hands dirty, instead overseeing the entire process and reporting directly back to my father, he decided to still dress for his former position. To any who looked at him wondering what he might do for a living, everything about his typical blue jeans and white tees screamed *mechanic* loud and clear.

Today, though, he had chosen a short-sleeved white tee seeing as it was all of thirty-three degrees out.

Manly men like him, apparently, did not require long sleeves.

When it came to Trip, I was inclined to believe he was kept warm by the hellfire lapping at his feet.

I had been hoping that, maybe, he would turn around, go back inside to tell my parents I was here finally. I had no such luck.

As soon as I cut the engine, he was jogging down the steps, making his way toward me.

"You're late." The words were out of his mouth as my feet hit the ground.

THERE BETTER BE PIE

And so it begins.

"Why, hello Trip. So glad to see you arrived safely," I added, tone dripping with sarcasm. "I am well aware I am late since I was stuck in bumper-to-bumper traffic because no one knows how to drive in the rain. I was absolutely *thrilled* to be on the road two hours longer than I planned."

"Your parents had to run out to grab potatoes."

"I stopped to pick them up!" I insisted, waving toward my back seat where the two five-pound bags were nestled.

"Yes, well, with no update from you, they had no choice but to assume you weren't going to make it. They weren't going to hold dinner forever."

Deep breaths. Do not murder the man with the tire iron so conveniently located under your front seat.

"It's illegal to text and drive," I reminded him.

"You could make a call."

"You've seen these roads around here, right? White-knuckle curves everywhere. I didn't think it was a good idea to get distracted and wind up wrapped around a tree. If you were so concerned about *my* parents having to run out to the store, you could have offered to go yourself," I reminded him, maybe taking a little too much pleasure in ramming my shoulder into his as I moved past, making my way toward my trunk.

"I offered. Your mother is far too good of a host to allow a guest to run to the store."

"Thank you, Trip. I did need a reminder of what kind of person my own mother is."

I maybe missed his face by all of two inches when I yanked the door of the trunk upward. And the bastard didn't so much as flinch.

"What? Are you moving in?" he asked, faced with my luggage carefully arranged to fit in the small space. I had every intention of completely ignoring that comment. But then he had to keep talking. "It's just the four of us,

THERE BETTER BE PIE

Princess. You didn't need to pack cocktail dresses and high heels."

"You're not family Trip, so you can't possibly know this, but we actually dress up for Thanksgiving. Even though it is—usually—just the three of us."

"Gee, you worried I can't keep up with your sense of style?"

"I do have a good sense of style," I told him, choosing to take the higher road on this one. "Thanks for noticing," I added. "No, I don't need your help," I insisted when he reached into the trunk.

"Sure you do. You might catch one of those skyscrapers on your feet in a hole in the ground while trying to drag these out and bust your face."

With that, and nothing else, he grabbed the two biggest suitcases, dragged them out as if they weighed nothing, and took off back toward the house like he owned the place.

Thankful for a moment alone, I took a deep breath, turning to look at the house.

When it comes to houses, the Maine house was my second favorite to the Pennsylvania Victorian where I had spent all my formative years.

Building-wise, it was a two-and-a-half story chalet-style house with sprawling porches on each of the first and second levels. There was just something about the steep pitch in the front and the floor-to-ceiling windows that made me think of snow and cups of hot cocoa, of the warmth of a fire and the comfort of loved ones close by.

The second-level deck off of the back overlooked the seemingly endless tree-lined lake, something we presumably shared with others somewhere along the lines, but somehow felt entirely our own at the same time.

There was a spot about half a mile through the woods where the shoreline jutted out a bit closer to the water. The previous owners must have thought it was as magical as I did because they had dragged giant smooth

THERE BETTER BE PIE

rocks from the waterline up to the spot, placing them in a circle around a stone fire pit.

I liked to take hikes through the woods in the very early morning before anyone else stirred, ending up in that space where I would uncover the fire pit—full of dry wood from the last time I visited—starting a cozy fire, and watching the sun move across the sky until the fire died down, bringing on the chill that would inevitably send me back toward the house for a shower and another coffee.

Going into my backseat for the couple extra bags I had there, I made my way up the uneven path—something my mother insisted added to its rural charm instead of evening them out—wobbling a bit on my toothpick heels. I couldn't help but wonder if Trip was standing there in the window, looking down on me with smug satisfaction that he was right about my choice of footwear.

Shaking off that thought, not wanting my mood to turn any more sour than it already was, I let myself in the front door, feeling like all my stress melted at my feet.

It would be difficult to hold onto my anger in a place that only had happy memories of laughter and delicious food and the occasional snow storm-watching from the living room directly inside the door.

It was a giant open floor plan with impossibly high ceilings with wooden beams criss-crossing the whole area.

The living room, in my opinion, had two major focal points. The giant stone and wood fireplace. And the floor-to-ceiling windows. The medium-brown sectional that I was pretty sure could comfortably seat an entire football team was positioned to mostly face the fireplace. But anyone who liked nature even in the least chose to sit on the side that also let you look out to take in the view. There was an ancient, enormous braided rug in reds, browns, grays, and beige on the floor under the large coffee table.

The entire space felt airy and never-ending.

To the other side of the living room was the kitchen in the same warm wood tones with a giant eight-burner stove, oversize fridge, and warm white countertops.

THERE BETTER BE PIE

As if anticipating I would bring the flowers despite her always telling me not to go out of my way, a beautiful crystal vase was already situated in the center of the island that was large enough for five people to prepare separate meals without getting in one another's way.

God, I loved this place.

From my position, I could see the overlook from the second story where Trip was bashing my luggage off of the railing as he moved down and out of sight.

I wasn't overly protective of possessions. My car had a few dings from accidentally opening the doors up into the cart return or ramming it with my cart itself. I wasn't exactly showy about my things. Yet my luggage set was a gift from my mother on my eighteenth birthday. Along with a plane ticket to Italy so I could get 'some culture' before I started college. It ended up being an important trip for me, a pivotal part of my maturity, a turning point in my life. So the luggage had sentimental value. And, well, it came from my mother which meant it had actual financial value as well.

Rushing up the stairs, careful not to trip, something I always secretly feared because the only thing in the house that I didn't like were the back stairs. Which, for God-knew-what reason, had no backs on them. I could always see myself accidentally slipping my foot through the back, getting trapped, falling backward, whacking my head, and dying right then and there.

Improbable? Yes.

But not entirely impossible either.

Whenever possible, I took the long way around to go back to the front staircase to avoid them entirely. But I wanted to catch Trip before he thumped my suitcases against the third set of stairs that led up to the final level of the house.

Which consisted entirely of my bedroom and bathroom.

It was meant to be the master suite, but my father said his knees didn't appreciate the extra set of stairs, so they had happily handed it off to me and taken one of the smaller rooms on the second floor.

"Just leave them there," I demanded just as he got to the staircase. "I have them from here."

"Can't have you carting them up the stairs all by yourself, can I, Princess?"

With that, he started up, leaving me following behind, trying my best not to imagine *him* being the one catching his foot, and whacking his head. "Stop grinding your teeth."

I didn't mind that order coming from my mother. Or even my father though he was usually not paying attention enough to notice I was doing it. It wasn't meant in a nasty way. In fact, it would likely save me on future dental bills.

But coming from Trip?

It seemed grumbly and demanding.

"It's annoying," he added. Which, well, in my mind, made it so I could officially think of him as an ass for saying it instead of wondering if he was just trying to give me a gentle reminder, and I was so intent on disliking him that I was going to take anything he said to me the wrong way.

"For someone who seems to find me so intolerable, you sure do find excuses to be around me more," I informed him as I made it to the landing, annoyed that I was a little out of breath and he was not. As if anyone would doubt that he would be the victor in a cardio competition—this man who looked like the Greeks used him as a model to create their statues. Whereas, it took a lot of time and effort in the gym and serious meal planning to keep my jeans fitting. And, let's face it, those jeans got super tight anytime I had more than a salad for dinner.

I wasn't the seventy-five pound heavier insecure wreck I once was, but I was no fitness model either.

Stairs got to me.

"I'm doing you a favor," he told me, gaze bored, indifferent.

"I didn't ask you for a favor," I reminded him. "In fact, I asked you twice to leave my luggage alone."

"You're in a mood," he observed. And it wasn't entirely untrue. Even if he was what had brought about said mood.

I was normally pleasant, damnit.

My friends—and even my boss—sometimes called me Sunshine because I was usually beaming and happy and warm.

I felt it said something about him that he was the only person on the planet who made me feel like I turned into an ice queen around him.

I hated this version of myself.

"Thank you for pointing that out," I told him, sucking my cheek between my teeth to keep from grinding again.

"No problem. Maybe go ahead and take a few minutes to put yourself together before your parents get back."

A million words rushed to the tip of my tongue then got tangled up together in one incomprehensible ball, leaving me sputtering as he turned to walk away.

Just as his feet were on the stairs, he called back, "And maybe take that stick out of your ass while you're at it."

Forget the *tragic* foot-catching accident.

I wanted to *throw* him down the stairs.

He was right about one thing, though, I did want to get myself together. I wanted a hot shower and a dry change of clothes.

That and a couple minutes alone, I hoped, would make it possible to deal with him until my parents returned.

On that, I opened up the door to my room, feeling another sigh of relief washed through me from my toes and up through the top of my head.

I had a view in the city, sure. Many people would kill to be able to wake up to a view in New York City.

But this?

THERE BETTER BE PIE

This was what I thought of when I heard the phrase 'a view.'

It overlooked the woods, the lake, the hills beyond them.

I always wanted to make a trip up here in the prime of autumn when all the trees were a blanket of reds and yellows and oranges.

Thanksgiving was always just two weeks too late, all the trees bare and stark against the landscape. Still breathtaking in their own way. And I was thankful for a reminder of the lovely things this house still had to offer. Even if I was sharing them with Trip Martin.

Much like the main room two floors below, my room had a vaulted ceiling with exposed woodwork, floor-to-ceiling windows, an earth-toned braided rug, and wooden floors. The queen bed butted up against the same wall as the door, facing the view, allowing me to wake up with the slivers of the sun in the early morning, giving me something beautiful to see as soon as my eyes opened. The bedding was pure whites mixed with brown and creme blankets and comforters.

The wall to the left of the door held the fireplace that would just barely keep me warm on the colder mornings. To the right was the door that led into the bathroom, one that featured a full-glass shower enclosure as well as the most luscious soaking tub I had ever seen in my life. If I knew the staff—and I did at this point—they would have gone over-the-top with fluffy towels, fancy hand soap, bath salts and bombs and bubbles in autumnal scents. It was unnecessary, but something I super appreciated too. I worked a lot in the city and didn't even *have* a bath. It was nice to be able to really indulge.

In my personal life, I didn't have anyone who worked for me. I often felt too guilty even to allow someone else to do my grocery shopping, and just pick it up when it was ready.

I still struggled not to feel guilty about the staff that my family employed, even though I had no control over

THERE BETTER BE PIE

that, and knew that my father had always been incredibly fair with salaries and benefits.

I had gone to private schools my entire childhood and adolescence, surrounded by kids just like myself. Born with silver spoons, given all the advantages in life. It never occurred to me to feel weird about our wealth.

It wasn't until I went off to college that I started to really see the wealth divide, started to grapple with some embarrassment about all the advantages I had in my life while others struggled.

My first year there, I asked my parents if I could sell the Kensley they had given me on my sixteenth birthday, taking that money to get myself a used sedan — the car I still drove around to this day—and sticking the rest in a savings account for my future plans.

I no longer bought designer clothes when things off the rack at Marshall's worked just as well. The stock I had in the family business was funneled into savings, never touched, forcing me to live off of the yearly salary just like everyone else.

My only indulgence, of course, was my shoes. Which I saved up for and indulged in with my spring bonus.

None of these things changed the fact that, no matter what happened with my life, I would never actually have to stress about money. But it allowed me to feel a little bit more average, more like my own person rather than my parent's daughter—just someone who lucked out.

Which was why I had a special little package tucked away with my clothes—a simple silver and gold wrapped box with a special little present to leave for Marta—the woman who took care of the inside of the house when we were not around—in gratitude for going that extra mile for me even though she really didn't have to.

Wiggling my shoulders to ease the ache there from so long in the car and, let's face it, interacting with Trip, I lifted my suitcases up on the bed.

There were two types of people.

THERE BETTER BE PIE

Ones who lived out of their suitcases on vacation. Then there were the freaks like me who had to unpack everything. Even though they knew they would need to repack everything in a few days.

What can I say, I had a vendetta against wrinkles.

As soon as everything was in the drawers and hanging in the closet, I grabbed a fresh outfit—yet again thankful that I always packed more than was necessary—and made my way into the bathroom, deciding to go with a shower, knowing that my parents should be back any minute, and not wanting to be rude by lounging in the tub.

Even if I was sure a bath would be a much better way to purge the interactions with Trip out of my system.

Twenty minutes later, my hair was dry, falling to my shoulders in a mix of brown and some carefully placed honey highlights around my slightly too round face. I went ahead and took the extra five minutes to apply the concealer and mascara I had longed for earlier, dragged on the cream sweater I had pulled out along with skinny jeans and beige heels.

A small spritz of perfume, and I felt ready to face Trip again.

I descended the stairs with a death grip on the railing, hearing the honey-sweet voice of my mother and the deep timbre of my father in the kitchen. I ignored Trip's somewhat annoyingly interesting gravel-sounding voice.

"Oh, honey! We're so glad you made it!" my mother cheered as soon as she saw me move into the room, hands releasing the flowers she had been separating to rearrange in her vase to move around the island and embrace me.

"I'm sorry I'm so late. The roads were awful this time."

"Don't apologize. We're just happy you're here. You really shouldn't have brought me flowers," she told me as I knew she would. "But they are absolutely beautiful."

"The beer," my father started while my mom's arms were still around me, "you absolutely should have. And

THERE BETTER BE PIE

thank you. Looks like there's enough if you want to share some with me too. If you've gotten over your thing."

My thing was a slight allergy that made my face feel all itchy when I tried to drink it. I knew he didn't mean to be so callous about it, that he genuinely just thought it was important to be able to share a beer with the people you care about, so I tried not to be offended.

"Well, I brought wine for Mom and me," I said instead, sending him a small smile.

My father was not who you imagined when you thought of old money. He was just shy of six feet with linebacker shoulders, a wide chest, a bit of a beer belly, a somewhat ruddy complexion with bright green eyes and a full head of salt and pepper hair.

He looked like your everyday man in his jeans and black long sleeve tee and tragic New Balance sneakers.

At least Trip, even being an every-day-Joe, had pretty impressive loafers on with his simple outfit.

In contrast, my mother—who was not from money—looked every bit the woman you might think of as old money. Not the cheaper new money full of lip injections and cheek fillers, but a gracefully aging woman closing in on her sixties. She was tall and lithe with the delicate bone structure I had always envied with bright blue eyes and blonde hair peppered with white.

She'd always possessed what I considered a timeless sense of style with her simple slacks or well-fitting jeans and tucked in long-sleeve button-ups in whites or stripes layered under oversized thick-knit cardigans in soft colors—grays, beige, pinks. She was wearing a white button-up with a golden cardigan today.

She did not share my love of heels and was wearing simple ballet flats in tan.

Never a fan of bold jewelry, she had pearls at her earlobes and a silver heart pendant necklace resting on her chest.

"Have you settled all in?" my mother asked. "Were there enough hangers in your closet?"

"You unpack on vacation?" Trip asked, brows furrowed.

"She's a curious one," my father said, shaking his head. "Well, let's go take some of these beers onto the deck while Katherine and Jett get dinner going."

"I can't help with anything?" Trip asked, looking over at my mom.

"No, no. You and Mitch go ahead and relax," she insisted, waving him off. "Thank you for offering, though." She waited for them to head outside before turning back to me with her usual sweet smile. "I told you he was a fine gentleman, Pudge," she said, and I was incredibly grateful that she hadn't let that old nickname slip in front of Trip.

There was no use explaining to her our less than cordial greeting. She would only find kind things to say about it.

"So, what are we making for dinner?" I asked, casting a glance over toward the porch, seeing my father clink his bottle of beer to Trip's.

Shaking off what I can only call a small bit of jealousy, I listened to my mother ramble off some recipe she'd seen in a magazine. Not Pinterest. My mother was old school. She subscribed to all the home and cooking print magazines known to mankind. She had half a dozen scrapbooks full of the winning recipes she'd found within.

With that, I cracked open our wine, rolled up my sleeves, and helped bring her Bruschetta chicken pasta and potato soup dreams come to life.

"What?" I asked when I found her shooting looks at me as I sipped my wine.

"Could I maybe talk you into making a tray of those amazing brownies of yours?" she asked, already grabbing the various items out of the fridge and pantry that I would need to make said dessert.

"I'd be happy to," I agreed, always glad to make her life a little easier by handling one part of the meal.

"Fantastic. Brownies are Trip's favorite."

THERE BETTER BE PIE

I kept the smile on my face while silently wondering if I could get away with slipping some laxatives into his slice.

"Great," I told her, getting to work.

An hour later, dinner was in our hands on the way to the dining room, and the brownies were in the oven.

The dining room was oddly placed on the other side of the house, a bit of a long walk from the kitchen, and I was acutely aware of the click-click-clicking of my heels on the floor the entire way there, swearing I could hear Trip's internal monologue about how obnoxious they were.

Proving I wasn't just paranoid, when we finally moved into the dining room where he and my father were situated, Trip's gaze was on my feet.

"Alrighty," my mom cheered, moving to place the hollowed-out bread bowl of soup in front of my father, leaving me to serve Trip. "Dig in," she added as I avoided all eye-contact as I dropped the bowl down, moving across the table to my spot. "So, how are things going with you guys and work?" my mom asked, and I resisted the urge to groan.

When it comes to touchy subjects between my father and me, his workplace was at the very top, right above my decision to register to vote for a different political party than him, and my adamant refusal to go fishing with him.

"Trip has really settled into his new leadership role. He is taking this company into the future."

Electric cars are not the future, Jett.

"That's so wonderful. We are so lucky to have you on the team, Trip," my mother agreed.

I don't want you to reinvent the wheel, Jett. No one actually cares about their footprint. It's all buzzword crap they know they are supposed to say while on their way to load up their giant SUVs at the gas station.

"I count myself lucky to work at your company," Trip said to my father, but I didn't miss the way his gaze slid to me after. As if to say *You're an idiot for not doing so yourself.*

"And Jett, how is your work going?" my mother asked, shooting a sweet smile in my direction. She wasn't just making polite conversation; my mother was always the sort who genuinely wanted to know.

"Jett fiddles on social media," my father supplied to Trip.

Fiddles.

I didn't care who you were, it stung a bit when one of your parents reduced your hard work to *fiddling*.

"I am in charge of marketing of an ethical and green cosmetics company," I corrected. "But it does involve some fiddling on social media," I added, giving my father a smile, not wanting to get into an argument, wanting to toe that very careful line we often did when interacting.

"Ethical meaning, what, employees get gold stars for participation and a crying room for when they're stressed out?" Trip asked, gaze piercing.

"Ethical meaning we don't strap down harmless animals and test products on them," I snapped, getting a glare from my father that told me he didn't appreciate me bringing up that subject.

Another sore spot.

I had once brought up this very topic in front of the CEO at a major—and *unethical*—makeup brand. I'd gotten a lecture like a ten-year-old after that one. About how some topics aren't to be discussed in mixed company.

"You did ask," I reminded Trip who at least looked a little chastened.

"I did," he agreed, going on eating.

My mother, bless her heart, charged on about fifty different topics over the next hour, keeping things light and airy, nothing controversial. I went ahead and only piped in when I knew for sure it would be safe to. Talking about how the city got during the winter, about what shows were currently running on Broadway that my parents might be interested in.

Trip managed to get a few more barbs in, but left me otherwise unscathed.

My family, good food, and my third glass of wine were making him a lot more tolerable than I expected.

Once or twice, I might have even felt the need to smile at something he'd said to my mother that had her beaming or that made my father laugh.

He seemed wholly capable of being charming and friendly to everyone else he encountered.

If everyone else can get along with him, Jett, did you ever stop to wonder if maybe it is you?

That was what my father had said after breaking up a particularly heated argument over—of all things—people bringing dogs to fireworks that my father was putting on in a public park to celebrate the Fourth of July.

I had taken the words to heart initially, until I remembered that I, too, got along with everyone else I came into contact with.

Trip and I were simply oil and water.

We didn't mix.

"Excuse me a moment," my father said, rushing off to answer his phone.

"No, please," Trip said, pressing a hand to my mother's as she reached for his plate. "Jett and I can get the dishes. You have done enough already. Right, Princess?" he asked, daring me to remind him that I, too, had helped make dinner.

"Right. I will happily do the dishes," I added, reaching to gather my father's along with my own. "Why don't you join my father on the deck?" I suggested to Trip.

"Nope. Got to do my part too."

I didn't even notice I had been grinding my teeth again until Trip fell into step beside me. "Stop."

"Just put them on the counter. I'll get them," I demanded, not mentally prepared to actually have to do dishes side-by-side with him.

He completely ignored me, going over to the sink, running the water.

THERE BETTER BE PIE

"What's with all the jabs at your father?" he asked, back to me as I moved the leftovers into a glass storage container.

"I don't know what you're talking about." I didn't, either. After a rocky start, the conversation had been pretty seamless.

"He tries his best to connect with you. And you shut him out."

"You don't know anything about my father and my relationship, Trip." I wanted the words to come out firm, but they had escaped a little sad even to my own ears.

"I know he wanted you to work at his company."

"I *did* work at his company," I reminded him. "I started in the mailroom when I was sixteen, and worked my way up."

"Then up and quit without notice."

He wasn't wrong.

But he didn't know why.

And I wasn't about to tell him.

"It was a family matter," I told him, watching as he shot me a raised brow for a moment before going back to his dishes.

"Regardless, you didn't have to be a brat and run off to New York instead of facing it up."

"You have a lot of opinions for someone who has no idea what he is talking about," I told him, watching as he shut off the water, turning to face me, mouth about to open.

"You two are the sweetest," my mother said, breezing in. "I hope you left room for dessert, Trip," she added, going over to start making a pot of coffee. "We have brownies."

"I'm sure I can squeeze in a brownie or two. You didn't have to make them for me, though, Kathy," he added, shaking his head.

"I didn't," she told him, coming up behind me, wrapping her arms around me. "Pudge did," she added.

Oh, God.

Yep.

THERE BETTER BE PIE

That just happened.

And judging by the way Trip's eyes were dancing, he was enjoying the hell out of it.

"Pudge?" he repeated, not even trying to hide his smile.

"Oh, that is Jett's old nickname. Pudge Muffin. She had this charming little muffin top," she added, pressing a hand to my belly, and drawing Trip's attention to a place that was still not my favorite part of my body.

With that, she moved off to collect the dessert plates.

"Pudge, huh?" Trip asked, lips twitching.

"Call me that again, and I'll kill you," I told him through a beaming smile, not wanting to upset my mother.

"Prefer Princess, huh?"

"I prefer my name, actually."

"Sucks then that you don't get to pick what people call you," he told me, turning to grab a cup of coffee. "Can I get you some coffee, Kathy?" he asked, pointedly not offering me one as he automatically made one for my father who took it black with one sugar just like he apparently did.

"Oh, no. I can't drink coffee after ten in the morning. It will keep me up all night. But thank you."

Trip turned, but didn't move away from the coffee machine, making me have to move in at his side to get my own cup.

It oddly annoyed me that, even in my six-inch heels, he still towered over me. I inherited nearly nothing from my mother. Not her blonde hair or her pale skin or her delicate build, and not her height either.

"Stop staring at me," I demanded, feeling his gaze looking down at the top of my head as I went about making my coffee. Two sugars, a dash of creamer, and a generous pour of sugar-free caramel syrup that my mother never forgot to have stocked for me.

"Get over yourself, Princess. I was watching the monstrosity you are making."

THERE BETTER BE PIE

"It's called coffee. Plenty of people put cream and sugar and syrup in their coffee. Especially because my father likes to drink the strongest coffee known to mankind."

"Sorry we didn't think to bring you a cappuccino machine, so you could make some half-caf, salted caramel, extra foam concoction."

"Oh my God. And you feel you have the right to criticize *me* for supposedly taking jabs at people? Can I just enjoy my coffee?"

"You can try," he agreed, nodding.

"Jett, honey, do you want dessert? Or are you being careful?"

I tried not to grimace, hating that turn of phrase. When I had first buckled down to lose some weight, she always sidestepped the term 'diet' though that was clearly what I was on at the time. Her favorite was always 'being careful' which never failed to make me feel like I was one bite away from being considered *careless* with my intake.

Not her fault.

It was my issue.

"Careful?" Trip repeated.

"Oh, Jetty tries to watch what she eats," my mom informed him while I prayed she let it drop at that. "I think those kids at school were a little judgmental when she had some extra padding on, right, honey?"

Judgmental was a nice way to put it.

Sure, my peers always understood that there was a sort of twisted hierarchy in school based on how rich our parents were, and that I was near the top behind a tech guru offspring, and the twins belonging to the owner of a giant pharmaceutical company. That meant that they always watched what they said in *front* of me.

Behind my back, when they thought I couldn't hear, though, that was a different story entirely.

Kids were cruel in general. It was a rule of life. But kids who had been raised to think that they could get away

THERE BETTER BE PIE

with anything they said simply because their parents were important people, yeah, they were sadistic little jerks.

"They weren't kind, that's for sure," I allowed, pushing those old feelings down again, reminding myself to keep them in the past where they belonged.

"Were you really that much bigger?"

Bigg-er.

Maybe it was a harmless word. Plenty of people would have used the same turn of phrase.

But coming out of Trip's mouth, well, I couldn't help but take offense.

Bigg-er.

Meaning he thought I was big now?

That certainly seemed like the inflection.

"Oh, I don't know. She was maybe four or six sizes bigger," my mother supplied. "But Jett has a wider build."

On that, my eyes closed tight for a long second, looking for a smidgen of confidence to face Trip again whose eyes I could still feel on me.

"Like her father?" he asked her but kept his gaze on me when I finally looked up at him again.

"Yes," I agreed, "like my father."

"Your father was..." my mother started.

"Please," I cut her off, turning, giving her my gaze which I knew had to have been desperate. "Can we change the topic?" I asked before she could spill it all.

"Are you feeling alright, honey?" she asked, brows lowering over concerned eyes. "You look a little flushed. Are you not feeling well? Your eyes are a bit small too."

"I think I have a headache coming on," I admitted, and it wasn't a lie.

"Oh, sweetie," she said, voice soft, knowing my history of sudden—and crippling—migraines. "Why don't you turn in early? We have plenty of time to catch up tomorrow. Take care of yourself. You had a long day," she added, pressing a kiss to my cheek before taking my father's coffee and brownie, heading out to bring it to him on the deck where he was still talking on his phone.

"Might not get headaches if you weren't always clenching your jaw."

To be fair, his tone, for a chance, wasn't overly condescending. Just observant. Just sharing an opinion.

But I was tired and a little too vulnerable at the moment.

"Where'd you get your medical degree?" I asked, glaring at him.

"Go get some sleep," he said, his own jaw tightening. "Maybe you will be pleasant in the morning. For a change. I won't hold my breath, though."

"Please do. This whole holiday would be a lot more tolerable if you suffocated," I added with a saccharine smile.

"Go to bed, Princess," he demanded, tone dismissive, a little cutting.

"Don't tell me wha—"

"Honey, go!" my mother insisted, waving a hand at me as she came back. "I will play hostess. Get some rest. You were up so early this morning. Go on. Up."

There was no arguing with my mother when she decided you needed to rest.

And, quite frankly, I wanted a break. A couple aspirin. And a good night of rest before I had to face Trip again.

"Dinner was great, Mom," I told her, giving her a one-armed hug.

"Dessert is great too," my mom assured me, even though she hadn't touched a brownie, never having been a huge fan of them. "Right Trip?" she prompted, and I caught him cutting himself another square.

"They're not bad," he allowed. "I'm surprised you bake."

"Oh, Jett is a great baker. She makes an amazing apple pie. You've just got to try it."

"Sure, I'd be willing to taste her pie."

Okay.

It was a nothing comment.

A throwaway, really.

Why, then, did it almost seem, I don't know, sexual?

And why in freaking hell did I feel an odd, completely unexpected, entirely absurd little spark of desire?

Tired.

I was clearly tired.

Maybe even a little delusional.

That was the only possible explanation.

Because there was no way in the world I could ever feel something even akin to desire toward a man like Trip freaking Martin.

CHAPTER THREE

Juliette

My parents were night owls by nature.

Me, I was always the early bird.

My eyes usually sprang open just when the sunlight was slicing through the darkness, reminding it that its time was over.

I wasn't someone who grumbled at the clock, who curled up in the blankets and tried to grab just five more minutes of sleep.

I didn't struggle to drag my mind together, to shrug off unconsciousness; I woke up fully all at once, ready to get moving.

And so I did.

My headache was gone.

Thanks to the impossibly soft mattress, so was the stiffness in my neck and shoulders.

I climbed out of bed, hastily throwing my hair into a ponytail, slipping into my wool-lined leggings, a long-sleeved tee, and a pair of walking shoes I left in the back of my closet for just this very purpose.

THERE BETTER BE PIE

My parents slept like the dead in the mornings, but I found myself tip-toeing down the stairs and through the house, not wanting to wake up Trip, refusing to allow him to ruin my perfect morning plans.

Grabbing a coffee in an insulated mug, I silently made my way outside just as the woods started to be illuminated, scaring off anything that might send me running and screaming.

There was nothing like this place, I decided each and every time I visited, taking slow, deep breaths that expanded both my belly and chest, pushing out all the exhaust fumes and smoke I breathed in on a daily basis back at home, replacing that with pine and dirt and water and the distinct, yet indescribable, scent of fallen leaves.

I never really seemed to follow the same path. Even if I wanted to, the woods changed too quickly to allow for such a thing given that I was likely the only person who ever trekked through them, and not nearly often enough to leave an actual trail through the underbrush.

I simply started off at one direction, using the lake as a point of reference, so I never got lost.

Walking had always been my preferred method of exercise. At my heaviest, it was really all I could manage cardiovascularly. When I did drop some weight, and my system could handle something more strenuous, I could never seem to consistently stick to anything else, preferring the peace I found in a good, long walk.

The city was full of walking. To and from work, to events, to the stores. But I always made time to walk through parks, to try to get some hints of nature even in the middle of a sprawling metropolis.

In the city, I walked with my cell or an iPod, needing to know how much time I was spending. And, let's face it, wanting a way to call for help should I need it.

In the woods, though, I refused to bring any electronics with me, not wanting any distractions, choosing to take the walk as a sort of meditation, a time when I could let go of everything that existed outside of this perfect, peaceful little sanctuary.

I had no idea how long I walked, only turning to head back when my thighs started to burn in objection at the idea of pushing it any further.

I made my way around the lake, bringing myself to my fire-pit, taking a moment to get it going, then settling down with my back against a rock, knees to my chest, staring off at the water as I finally started to drink my coffee.

"You get up early."

"Jesus!" I shrieked, hand flying over my heart as my head whipped around, finding an interloper in my personal paradise.

Not my parents, of course.

I wasn't so lucky.

Nope.

It was Trip, looking fully rested even at this hour, dressed in a pair of black basketball pants with double white stripes down the sides, sneakers, and a gray sweatshirt, his hair a little mussed, his face a bit flushed.

"Didn't mean to scare you. I wasn't exactly quiet walking up."

"I wasn't paying attention," I admitted.

"Smart. In the woods. There are bears in here, you know."

"You don't say," I mumbled, trying not to let him get a rise out of me. It was too early to get annoyed at the day.

"I was on the other side of the lake. Saw the smoke. Didn't realize there was a fire-pit here." He told me this as he invited himself to join me, taking the rock chair beside mine, entirely too close. I could feel the heat radiating off of his body.

"What were you doing in the woods this early?" I asked, making sure my tone was calm and conversational even if all I wanted to do was tell him to leave me alone.

"Going for a run," he admitted. "Your mom... she cooks heavy," he added with a little chuckle.

She did, that.

I never blamed her for my weight issues as a kid, but all the butter and pasta didn't help, I was sure.

"Yeah, you look like you need to be watching your figure," I drawled.

"Wow, Princess. That sounded dangerously close to a compliment."

"It wasn't one," I insisted.

"I'm taking it as one," he told me, leaning back, stretching his legs out, more at ease, more agreeable in the morning.

But only by a little bit.

And only in theory.

I wasn't actually *enjoying* his company.

But, you know, maybe somebody else might.

"I see why you like it here. This is a great spot."

"Private," I agreed, maybe a little pointedly.

"Your father never mentioned this when he was telling me about the property."

"He might not know it exists. He's not much of an explorer."

"There it is again."

"There what is again?"

"A dig."

"It wasn't a dig. It's a fact. He likes his creature comforts and things that are familiar to him. He's not someone who goes trekking through the woods looking for a fun new spot. That's not who he is. And that is not a dig. And, newsflash, he's my father. I get to say whatever I want about him."

"Not if it's negative. Not in my presence."

"He's a grown man, Trip. If he needed to defend himself, he could do it. He doesn't need you to speak for him."

"He's not here to defend himself."

"There was nothing to defend him about!"

THERE BETTER BE PIE

"You clearly have some issues with him, Princess. You're not even subtle about it."

"Oh, my God. Trip. Don't think you can come in here and play shrink. This is my family, not yours. Is that why you're here? Your own family can't stand you either? Not even your own mother? I mean, it's not a surprise. You'd be hard even for a mother to love."

"My mother died last month," he told me, voice a barely-healed wound scratched open.

The words landed like a slap, shocking me back, leaving pain in their wake.

My mouth sputtered as my heart crushed. I wasn't a cruel person. I didn't say things to hurt others. I didn't rub salt in open wounds.

I felt like the biggest bitch in the world.

An apology worked its way up my throat. But as I finally found the words, Trip was gone, nothing but a solid back steadily making his way as far from me as possible.

This time, I couldn't even blame him.

I couldn't have known. Of course not. We weren't exactly Facebook friends. We didn't run in the same circles, talk to the same people. There was no way I could have heard about his mother's passing.

Save for my father.

Who had to have known.

And if he knew, so must my mom.

Why the hell wouldn't they tell me that?

My special place ruined with the scene, I got up, making my way back to the house, soul a little heavy.

I couldn't imagine losing my mother. And I had known him to be close with his own, often bringing her to the work events instead of a date.

She'd been an older lady, making Trip a late-in-life baby. But I hadn't thought of her as old enough to have been at risk of dying. Then again, death was an equal opportunity bastard, stealing the young and the old alike.

"Mom," I hissed when I ran into her in the kitchen making her coffee, somehow managing to make a floor-

THERE BETTER BE PIE

length floral robe look like couture. "How could you not tell me that Trip's mom died?" I asked, keeping my voice low.

"Oh, honey. It's so sad, right? I didn't feel it was my place to share his personal business. That was why your father invited him up. He doesn't have any other family. When his mom passed, he was completely alone in the world."

Suddenly, I started to understand his almost irrational need to defend my father even when I wasn't even saying anything nasty about him.

My father acted as a sort of surrogate father to him. He'd taken Trip under his wing years before, beefing him up, teaching him all the things he'd never taught me about the inner workings of the business, treating him very much like the son he'd never had.

Of course Trip had latched onto that.

I couldn't really even blame him. And I was trying really hard to find a reason to.

"Why? What happened? Did you say something about her? Was he upset?"

"Yeah, you could say that," I admitted, closing my eyes, leaning down on the island to cover my face with my hands.

"Oh, no. Honey, you have to make that right. He must be heartbroken. You're not usually so callous."

"I wouldn't have been had I known!" I insisted, dangerously close to crying. It was one thing to have a social faux pas. It was a complete other to tell some guy that his dead mother didn't love him.

God.

"He came in right before you. Go apologize, honey. Before too much time passes. You'll both feel better."

She was right.

I had to apologize.

My stomach was twisted in painful knots.

I had to say the words, get them off my chest.

Even if I had to say those words to freaking Trip Martin.

"I'm going," I agreed, taking a deep breath, moving off toward the stairs.

I knocked.

And knocked.

Finally, knowing he was in there, I reached to push the door open, freezing for a cripplingly long moment at finding him sitting off the end of the bed, forehead in his hands.

For a soul-crushing second, I thought he might be crying.

But then his hand dropped.

His head lifted.

And there were no tears in his eyes.

Oh, no.

There was a burning rage.

"Trip, I'm so sorry," I told him, and no one could doubt the sincerity in my tone. "I had no idea."

"Clearly."

"I didn't... I'm not that callous."

"Telling someone their mom doesn't love them is a shit thing to say, Princess. Even if they are alive," he told me, getting to his feet. Was it possible for someone to do something like that angrily? Because if it was, that was what he did.

He stalked over toward me, footsteps like cannons in the quiet house.

He seemed like he was about to barrel right into me, making me take a hasty step back, my heartbeat skittering. For one second, I might have even worried he might strike out even though I knew in my heart he wasn't *that* kind of asshole.

"Trip, I'm sorry."

"So you said," he growled, grabbing the door, and slamming it in my face.

So much for making it right, smoothing it over.

Somehow, we went from Trip being the jerk, to it being—undeniably—me.

THERE BETTER BE PIE

Suddenly, words came back to me from my childhood, when I had been sobbing in my mother's arms because my best friend didn't want to be my best friend anymore because we had argued.

Sorry is all you can say, Pudge. But that doesn't mean that it's enough.

Clearly, it was not enough.

It was going to be a long, long day.

And it was going to be several hours before I could turn to alcohol to ease the sting of it all.

After a long shower where I tried to convince myself that it would all be okay, that I would go out of my way to be kind to Trip—even if he was being a complete tool—that I could still make this right and salvage this holiday, I made my way downstairs to find my parents and Trip already at the dining table enjoying the simple spread of eggs and toast my mother had quickly thrown together.

I made my way to my empty seat, reaching for a slice of toast.

And Trip promptly excused himself. Despite having a half-filled plate.

"What did you say to Trip?" my father asked, and there was no mistaking the accusation in his eyes.

"Something I never would have said if someone would have told me about his mother's passing," I shot back, face starting to burn.

Almost no one had the ability to actually make me blush in embarrassment. My father was one of the very few who could manage it with a simple *look*.

Everyone knew that look.

It was the *I am so disappointed in you* look.

"You said something about his *mother*?" he hissed, eyes nearly as angry as Trip's had been an hour before.

"I already apologized," I told him, holding up a hand to fend off the lecture.

"Clearly, not well enough," he shot back. "If you'll excuse me, I seem to have lost my appetite as well."

THERE BETTER BE PIE

Alone with my mother, my hand rose to cover my eyes.

"Everything is going wrong, and I haven't even been here a whole day yet," I told my mom, fiercely blinking back the tears that were forming. I wasn't going to cry. I wasn't going to make a bad situation worse. With my luck, Trip would see and then accuse me of making the situation about myself.

"The day is young, sweetie," my mother comforted, reaching out to pat my other hand with hers. "There is plenty of time for it to get better."

My mother, the optimist.

As it turned out, though, things did not get better. Not with both Trip and now my father angry at me, refusing to be near me, to listen to my apologies.

I was not a silent treatment kind of person. I would much rather have the uncomfortable conversation, get it out in the open, get it out of our minds and hearts than let it fester and punish someone else with my silence.

My father and Trip, though, were not of the same mind.

I was given the cold shoulder.

And because I refused to try to make my mom choose between us, I just encouraged her to go hang out with them.

While I went ahead and had a drink. Or two. Or three.

I lost count.

But somewhere along the way, after avoiding dinner, claiming I wasn't hungry—which everyone knew was a lie—I somehow got the idea that slipping into my bathing suit, and wrestling off the cover to the hot tub would be a good idea.

At least it was an excuse not to be around anyone else and deal with their painful silence. And my mother's equally painful attempts to get everyone to include me when they clearly did not want to.

THERE BETTER BE PIE

I took a long drink out of the entire bottle of wine I brought out to the hot tub with me, then sat back, closed my eyes, and tried to enjoy the floating feeling of drunkenness, hoping it was strong enough to numb all the other feelings coursing through me.

"Alright," a voice said, cutting through my floaty little half-dreamworld, dragging me back into the ugly reality, knowing that voice, knowing who it belonged to.

Trip.

"I think you've been punished enough," he added, making my eyes open to find him standing there on the deck above me, dressed only in a pair of low-slung black bathing trunks that put his annoyingly perfect abs on display, complete with that enviable deep V of his Adonis belt.

Bathing trunks, though, meant only one thing.

He was coming in.

Then, just as that thought formed, he did, slipping down into the water, making me acutely aware of how small a hot tub really was. And how intimate it felt to share what was, essentially, a bath with someone else.

"The silent treatment is immature," I managed to inform him, a little loose lipped when I was drinking. If I thought it, I usually said it. It was a miracle that I managed to keep the parts about his body inside my head only. "They consider it a form of abuse actually," I added, giving him a nod when his brow rose.

"You're a talk-shit-out person."

"It only hurts you when you let things fester."

"That's fair enough," he agreed, looking off toward the woods for a long moment, searching for what to say, how to start. "My mom was all I had," he told me. "Losing her was like losing a part of myself."

"I can't imagine," I admitted, feeling the tears I had been fighting filling my eyes at the knowledge that someday—hopefully *very* far down the road—I would absolutely wouldn't have to imagine. Just the idea of that was like a knife sliced through my insides.

"Don't," he demanded, voice rough when his gaze moved back to me. "Can't take tears right now, Princess."

"I won't judge you if you cry too," I told him, reaching up to swat tears away.

I wouldn't, either.

Having grown up with a typical man's-man who seemed allergic to open displays of emotion, I came to really appreciate the men I met in college who felt comfortable enough to admit that they got sad and overwhelmed and teared up too.

To that, he gave me a strained sort of smile. "I don't cry."

"Everyone cries. Even if they don't do it in public."

"I don't cry," he repeated. "I had no old man growing up. Even though my mother would never put the burden on me, little boys of single moms, they see themselves as the man of the family. I had to be strong for her. I stopped crying when I was seven. And only then because I broke my leg in three places."

"Well, in case no one has ever told you, it's okay to cry. Especially over the big stuff."

"I'll keep that in mind," he agreed, though I knew it was in one ear and out the other. "You're not such a pain in the ass when you're drinking, huh?" he asked.

I wasn't so drunk that I didn't feel the fizzle of anger. I *was* so drunk that it was quickly drowned in happy nothingness.

"You're almost tolerable when I'm drinking," I agreed, feeling my smile curve up.

"I concede that I was maybe being a dick earlier."

"Just earlier? Or do you maybe mean the past several years?"

"You've been no picnic yourself," he told me, shaking his head.

"To my reco-reco... that's a hard word," I told him, trying to force it to the tip of a tongue that suddenly felt a little fat and slow. "Rec-o-llection. What was I saying?"

To that, his lips twitched. "You were trying to blame me for every one of our arguments. Even though you are a pain in the ass too."

"Right. Well, I recall that you have started most of our disagreements."

"The way I remember it, you took everything I said out of context."

"Memory is funny," I said, nodding. "Like how yours is clearly always wrong."

"Agree to disagree then," he said, shrugging a shoulder. "Maybe we can call a truce. Just for the holiday," he clarified. "For your parents' sake."

"That might be a good idea," I agreed. "My father is pissed enough at me, I think."

"I think you may get your temper from him."

"That depends."

"Depends?" he asked, brows furrowing.

"On whether you subscribe to the nature or nurture mindset."

One more thing I could always count on alcohol for. Loose lips.

"What are you talking about?"

"He's not my biological father," I told him.

"Wait... what?" he asked, shaking his head. "I saw pictures of him with your mom in the hospital room after you were born."

"Yeah, he was there," I agreed. "But have you ever, I don't know, taken a look at me?"

"Yeah, Princess, I've looked at you."

Something about the way he said it made my belly wobble in a way that was too delicious. Clearly, this was another side effect of drinking. One I'd never had before. But there was no other explanation.

"Well, then you've noticed that I have dark hair and a round face and a stockier build."

"Christ, you're not stocky, Jett."

"I'm not bashing myself. I'm just not... you know... delicate like my mother. And I have brown eyes," I added.

THERE BETTER BE PIE

"Plenty of people don't look like their parents."

"I do, though," I told him. "I am the spitting image of my paternal grandmother. On my biological father's side. The same round face, high cheekbones, honey brown eyes, more olive skin."

"This is a weird question, but does your father... does *Mitch* know?"

"That he's not my father?" I clarified with a smirk. "I think it would have been hard not to know seeing as my mom was seven months pregnant with me when they married."

"You can't just let the story drop there. Is it a big secret?"

"No. I mean... my mom explains a big part of her story every Christmas to a bunch of people. I don't think she'd mind if I told you."

"Are you going to?" he asked when a long moment passed.

"Oh, right. Well... where to start."

I guess the start, when it came to my mom and the man who came to be my father in every way but genetics, meant I had to go all the way back to middle school. Where they'd met.

My father had been new in town, having failed out of his third prep school. His parents—the socialites they were—had a bit begrudgingly taken him back, enrolled him in the local public school as punishment, and all but washed their hands of him, leaving him mostly to be raised by the house and groundskeepers.

Unfortunately for them, my father didn't take public school as a punishment. In fact, he started to thrive. Then he developed an all-consuming crush on my mother. Who didn't want anything to do with him.

"Believe it or not, way back then, my mother was someone who had a thing for the bad boys," I told Trip, shaking my head. Even knowing how her story went down, even knowing her patterns, I found it really hard to imagine my sainted mother wanting anything to do with the typical muscle-car-driving, cigarette-smoking- heavily-partying, bed-hopping bad boys.

So he went ahead and became her friend, just wanting to be near her even if she didn't share his feelings.

All through high school, she would fall for some tool, become obsessed with him, get pulled around by the heart, then brutally dumped. And my father would be there to help put her back together, build her confidence back up. Then off she went to the next guy.

It was their toxic pattern.

And, as much as I hated to think anything negative about my mother, it was unkind of her to string him along when she knew all along his feelings were different than hers.

"She's not responsible for his feelings, though," Trip told me, surprising, and I realized that maybe I had painted him in my mind as someone shallow, when there was actual depth to be found there.

"No, you're right. And I think her past traumas and unstable family life made it easy for her to fall for these jerks who reminded her of her own absentee father."

After graduation, though, they both went off in different directions. Adulthood was calling for drastically different paths for the two of them.

My father went off to Cambridge, attending his father's Alma Mater, doing what was expected of him by getting his business degree, so that he could come back and run the company.

My mother, however, followed a flame out to California where he promptly dumped her, leaving her to attempt to juggle community college classes in design as well as waitressing and trying to pay her bills at the ripe old age of eighteen.

Much to her credit, even bouncing from bad relationship to bad relationship, she did get her degree, and was even planning on opening up her own little business.

"Then she met my father. My biological father," I clarified.

THERE BETTER BE PIE

Honestly, my mother had never given me a lot of information about him. Aside from the fact that he was an electrician who had been working on her apartment building at the time. I wasn't sure how things progressed, how they got to the point where they were living together, and she was suddenly not working, relying on him for everything.

"Just the cycle of abuse, I guess."

She finally found a guy who told her he loved her, that he'd take care of her, that he would never let her get away.

Where many of us would have heard sirens and seen red flags, all she saw was the hurt little girl who just wanted to be loved, had never healed from that early abandonment.

So she fell into him, into his life. It became all she knew. It isolated her. It twisted her thinking in such a way that she believed him when he said he was sorry after leaving bruises, that he would never do it again.

She lived like that for two years, hardly ever leaving their apartment, waiting on him hand and foot, giving up any dreams she'd ever had for her own life and future.

"And then the stick turned blue."

It was a new prison, another rope tying her to a man who would show her nothing but misery.

"But it also gave her more freedom than she was used to. Suddenly, she had all these appointments to go off to. And my father would let her use the car because he couldn't be bothered to take her himself."

It was on one of those outings, when she'd been treating herself to a hot chocolate with some money she had found forgotten under his front seat, that she happened to run into a familiar face.

"She told me that running into him again at that point in her life was like seeing him clearly for the first time."

THERE BETTER BE PIE

They'd talked for hours before she realized she needed to get home, knowing she was going to get into a fight when she did for being gone so long.

"Dad said he saw something when they were parting, that there was a fear in her eyes that he didn't feel comfortable with. So he, ah, followed her home without her knowing."

He admits it was a creepy move, that normal people didn't react that way.

"He was worried about his childhood crush," Trip said, shrugging.

"Yeah. And I think we can all agree that it was the right move. My biological father seemed ready to kill her—and me—that night."

My father could never really tell me what happened in those moments after he burst through the door, drawn by the sounds of her screams, but my mother told me that he'd nearly beaten my biological father to death that evening.

"Then he had turned to my mom, pulled her off the ground, and told her that she was coming home with him."

"And she did," Trip guessed.

"And she did," I agreed.

There had been no romance at first. She'd simply moved in with him back in their hometown, recovering physically, healing mentally and emotionally, taking care of herself so she could take care of me when I came.

"And in that healing, I think she saw what she had been too damaged to see before. That my father was always who she was meant to be with. When she finally came to that conclusion, they decided to stop wasting time, to get married, to raise me together."

"That's quite a story."

"Yeah. It's why the two of them eventually opened the women's shelter."

"You guys spend Christmas there, right?"

"Yeah. We bring gifts from the wish lists—and add some things in for the moms too—and sneak them under the tree. Then we stay behind to cook and serve a big meal so

THERE BETTER BE PIE

the rest of the staff can go home to their families. Thanksgiving is really our only family-only holiday."

I continued, "Well, that and the pie. And the fact that gifts aren't required. I am a terrible gift-giver."

"Really?"

"It's not that I don't try! I spend all year trying to find something good. But I never manage it. I am not one of those people who seem to pick out the absolute best gift for a person. And then I feel awful about my less-than-spectacular gifts. And it ruins it for me. I like that Thanksgiving is only about food and togetherness. No expectation of anything else."

"Adjusting to holidays without family is going to be rough," he admitted. "Maybe I'll find somewhere to volunteer too."

"I'm sure my father would be happy to have you at the shelter."

"Just your father?"

"Well," I said, smirking. "Maybe my mother too."

He let out a small chuckle. "You'd like it, I think. It's nice to give back. It means a lot to my mother. Plus, you do still get to do some shopping and wrapping, so you can be in the spirit."

"You guys spend the whole day there?"

"We head out late that night, meeting back at my parent's house to indulge in some extra sweets."

"You don't exchange presents at all?"

"No. We really don't need anything. Well, my dad always gets my mom something. But other than that, no. What did you and your mother usually do? The whole big meal and baked goods and giant pile of presents thing?"

"Well, we always had a big meal. But my mother was a horrible cook. Ever since I was a kid, we always ordered enough takeaway on Christmas Eve to feed an army, then just ate that all through Christmas day."

"Wait... what did you do on Thanksgiving if your mom didn't cook?"

THERE BETTER BE PIE

"We went out on Thanksgiving to eat. So we generally got a lot of the same things."

But restaurant Thanksgiving wasn't homemade Thanksgiving. It didn't give you the endless servings so that you couldn't fit another bite, so that your pants got too tight, so that you needed to shuffle the few feet over to the living room and drop down on the couch for a nap.

It was sweet that they had their own traditions, but I had to admit that I was maybe even a little bit excited for him that he would get to experience a more traditional Thanksgiving celebration. It would have been too depressing to imagine him sitting alone at a restaurant on Thanksgiving. Sure, he would still be missing his mother while he was here with us, but at least he wasn't on his own.

"Are you excited to have a home-cooked Thanksgiving?"

"Yeah. Your mom is a good cook."

"If you thought these last few meals were good, you're in for a real treat tomorrow. She gets up at four a.m. to get started. We are usually eating around three in the afternoon. And then usually hitting it all again later. And *then* dessert."

"I'll feel guilty sitting on my ass while she runs around cooking."

"We."

"Hm?"

"We. I cook too. I am usually up right after her. We both get to work on the baking first, always trying to outdo each other on the pies. And then we get started on the meal."

"No parade?"

"We take breaks to glance at it. And we always take a minute for the end."

"What does Mitch do?"

"Watches the games. Tells us that everything smells good. Drinks beer. We don't mind it being a traditional gender roles thing. It's nice to be able to have some time alone with my mom to cook. We used to cook together all

THERE BETTER BE PIE

the time when I was home. I'm happy to eventually get back."

"Get back?"

"To Pennsylvania. That was always my plan. Get my career in order. Save some money. Then move back home, find a fixer-upper, make it my own. Maybe host Sunday dinners with my family."

"Save money," he scoffed, eyes rolling.

"Yes, save money. To buy a house."

"Princess, you have stock in the company. And a trust fund."

We were back to Princess, back to that cool tone he so often used with me.

"Yes," I agreed, reaching for the wine once again, feeling the buzz slipping away, my shoulders lifting, my jaw tightening. "I have stock. I believe you have stock as well, so I don't know why you have that tone about it."

"I saved up and bought into it."

"And because I was gifted it, you get to look down on me."

"No one said I look down on you."

"Your tone implies it."

"You're inferring things based on your own insecurity."

"I'm defensive," I corrected, not wanting to admit my own insecurity, my own issues with imposter syndrome. "Since you seem to think you are better than me because you weren't born wealthy."

"I believe in hard work."

"And I work hard, Trip." My voice was loud, my tone sharp.

"After turning your back on the family business."

"You don't know what you're talking about."

"I know your father believes in the family legacy."

"But he never believed in me." The words were out before I could stop them, landing hard and heavy, making me wish I could suck them right back in, bury them back where I'd been keeping them for years.

"What are you talking about?" Again, that cold tone, that condescension.

Something in me snapped—my ability to control myself, to keep in all the ugly I had been harboring for years.

"You think I didn't want the legacy? That I didn't pin all my hopes on it? That I didn't believe it was my future? I wanted it. I started working at the company as soon as I was able to. Everything seemed fine. But he hated everything I suggested, shot down every single idea I ever came to him with about the future of the company. He didn't want me to take over. I wasn't what he had in mind."

"What do you mean you weren't what he had in mind?"

"He wanted a son, Trip," I shot back, flinging my wet hair over my shoulder. "The company always went from father to son. That was how it worked. He wanted a son. A true heir to the Kensley family."

"Jett..."

"But he couldn't have an heir," I charged on, barely registering the sudden softness in his voice. "Because of me."

"What do you mean because of you?"

"While delivering me, my mom had a uterine rupture. I slid out of her uterus and into her belly. The only way they could stop the bleeding was to remove the uterus. Making it impossible for her to give him an heir."

"Jett, come on," Trip said, shaking his head. "It wasn't your *fault* that they couldn't have more kids."

"Any," I corrected. "They couldn't have any kids."

Though, of course, I knew it wasn't actually my fault. It was a freak happenstance due to the fact that my mother had scars from getting fibroids removed in her early twenties. No one could have known. Had they known, they would have insisted on a C-section which would have made it possible for my mother to carry again, though she would always need to have a C-section in the future.

It was just a tragic situation.

THERE BETTER BE PIE

For her.

For the family they had wanted to build.

"Come on, you think that Mitch doesn't think of you as his daughter? He loves you. He raised you. What?" he asked when my gaze fell, trying to hide the pain I knew was in my eyes.

"He loved my mom. I was just part of the deal."

"Oh, fuck off with that," he snapped, making my gaze shoot up. "I get that you maybe would have insecurities about the whole situation. As a kid. But you're a grown woman, Jett. Mitch loves you. Him not liking your ideas has nothing to do with him not being biologically related to you."

"He loves all your ideas," I told him, knowing it was true because my father gushed about them all the time when we got together.

"Because we think the same way, have the same idea of where the company is going. It has nothing to do with blood, Jett, or even that I am, what, the son he never had. It's about having the same vision. We think alike. You don't."

"That's why you act all superior? Because you think like him when I don't?"

"I don't act superior, Princess."

"And yet you insist on calling me that."

"You were born a princess, Jett. As close as you could be in this country. You grew up without a care in the world. You never had to struggle. You are the only heir to this insane empire."

"I didn't choose any of that." And I absolutely had my own struggles.

"No," he agreed, nodding. "But you did choose to be a brat and leave without notice, run off to a new town."

"A brat?" I snapped, anger bubbling up hard and fast, replacing any of the remaining bits of sympathy I felt for the man. "Excuse me, but you have no idea what led to my leaving."

"I know that your father felt blindsided. And walked around the place in a daze for weeks, unsure what to do, who would fill that void."

"And you so helpfully stepped into that place, didn't you?"

"Someone had to."

"It's pretty rich that you look down your nose at me for being born rich, yet you think being an opportunist is somehow superior."

"I worked to get to my position, Princess. Did your sudden absence leave an opening for me? Yeah, it did. And it doesn't make me an opportunist. It meant I was in the right place at the right time and had the right skill set to provide what was needed. You can be a child about it and think that your father would just leave the space open indefinitely if you want, but I would suggest you grow up already, have a conversation with your father, and get over your issues."

With that, he rose up out of the water.

And, damnit, I looked.

I more than looked.

I watched the way his muscles flexed in his stomach as he unfolded his long body, as the water trickled down between each ab, followed the steam as it rose up off his skin.

I looked for long enough that my mind got wiped of anything even halfway intelligent to say, anything snarky to snap back.

Then without another word, he briskly made his way back into the house, stealing my towel as he went.

As for me, I went ahead and drank away the undeniable pressure in my lower belly that I knew well enough to call the oppressive sensation of unfulfilled desire.

Not toward him, of course.

Just in general.

I couldn't even recall the last time I'd been with a man. It had to have been over a year at that point. And my body was simply responding to the sight of a body of the opposite sex, forgetting it belonged to the most impossible person I'd ever met.

I attempted to drink away, as well, the knowledge that he'd had several points, no matter how fervently I was attempting to deny it.

I *had* left the family business without notice, without even saying much of anything about it. I had run away from responsibilities instead of facing them up.

I have also cradled resentment over the whole situation to my chest in the years following, despite having played a hand in creating the problem.

And, yes, I have even been carrying with me a deep well of insecurity about not being a legitimate heir, about being a sort of consolation prize. A child, yes, but not a biological one, not the one I knew he had wanted.

Yet I have never heard my father say anything of the kind.

He'd always cared for me like his own, showered me with anything I wanted, encouraged me when it was needed, punished me when necessary.

My feelings of being an interloper, of being illegitimate, those were my own issues, things I had buried down instead of facing, instead of working through.

It was time to work on that, to have that tough conversation, to lay it all out there—raw and bleeding—and seek healing instead of new ways to hide the pain.

Not over this weekend.

I didn't want to ruin the holiday any more than it already was.

With an empty bottle in my hand, and the promise of an epic hangover waiting for me in just a few short hour's time, I climbed out of the hot tub, trying to shake off some of the water so I didn't drip all through the house, then quickly making my way inside, shivering, once again cursing Trip as I stripped out of my bathing suit, wrapped myself in my blankets, and fell into a dead sleep, wondering what way he might get under my skin the next day.

CHAPTER FOUR

Trip

It was no secret how much I respected Mitch Kensley.

All the way back to that first day at work, just a low man on the totem pole, helping to put these amazing cars together.

I had, as many young boys did, been obsessed with cars as far back as I can remember, always begging my mother to let me get those ninety-nine cent toy cars at the grocery store whenever there was a little money to spare.

The older I got, the more into them I got. Especially after my grandfather who I'd never been close with because—as my mother put it—he 'liked the bottle more than us,' died, leaving me a piece of junk old pick-up truck— more rust than metal with an engine full of leaves and rotting hoses—which I knew to be the only possible way I would ever get a car of my own.

My mother had agreed to let me keep it if I found the money to replace the parts myself.

A passion was born on that long summer when I got myself a job helping out at a local shop, making money to fix up my truck while keeping an ear open, keeping my eyes peeled, soaking up any information the mechanics were willing to give me.

From there, I rebuilt that truck, sold it, got another, rebuilt it, sold it.

Eventually, I graduated from being a shop errand boy and tire-plugger to an actual mechanic, eventually taking some classes to make it more official, to give me a leg-up on a more secure future.

Job security was most easily found at the dealerships.

And there was no better dealership than that of Kensley Automobiles.

Honestly, I had applied to the position on a lark, never thinking I had a snowball's chance in hell at even getting a call back, figuring they only wanted truly seasoned hands, people who knew every in and out of luxury cars. I'd spent my limited career on trucks and old muscle cars. My hands had never touched a Mercedes, let alone a Kensley.

The answer is always no if you don't ask, Bubba.

That was my mother encouraging me to apply.

I knew they would love you. How could they not?

That was her when I came home in a state of shock to tell her that they'd offered me the job.

Me, some nobody twenty-something.

They wanted me to work on their fancy cars that were only available to the mega-rich and ultra visible.

And they wanted to pay me a really high salary and benefits package for the honor.

From day one, Mitch Kensley came off to me as this larger-than-life person, someone who sat on millions of dollars, but still chose to come into work every day, someone who took pride in his business, in his relationships with the men and women who made it possible.

I'll admit that he became a sort of father figure to me from the moment he introduced himself to me, guided me, brought me under his wing, showed me all the things there were to love about Kensley cars.

THERE BETTER BE PIE

My father had been a run off, someone allergic to responsibilities, never to be seen or heard from again.

While my mother and I had always had a close relationship, there was no denying that I had longed for a steady, strong male role model growing up.

In Mitch, I found that.

In me, I guess maybe he *did* find that sort of father-son connection.

I didn't agree with Jett that her dad resented her or didn't think of her as his own. If that was the case, it would have been known that she was not actually his. Instead, only the close family seemed to be aware of that fact.

Mitch loved Jett.

But she'd never—at least when I had known her—been in love with cars, in the luxury lifestyle these particular cars represented.

The first time I had seen her around the building, she'd charged into Mitch's office in those ridiculous high heels of hers, wearing striped pants and a white tee that tied in the middle, smiling huge as she told her father that the local gas station had installed an electric car charging station.

She'd been, well, beaming.

Bright, happy, lively.

Beautiful.

"I told you electric was making strides!" she'd gushed, kissing his cheek.

"What do you think about electric, Trip?" he'd asked, making her gaze slide to me for the first time. Curious, maybe a little intrigued.

"Electric is never going to be a thing," I told him. Partly because I believed it to be true. Electric was too expensive for the average consumer. And most wealthy people didn't care too much about their footprints as they flew in their private jets to the palatial estates that they only stepped foot in for one week every year. The other part, though, was because I knew Mitch didn't think there was a future in it, and wanting him to like me.

THERE BETTER BE PIE

It was right there, in that moment, when I'd unwittingly made an enemy.

She'd hated me immediately, avoided me, excused herself from conversations when I'd joined in.

It wasn't long before it started to get under my skin. Which, in turn, made me want to get under hers as well.

I wasn't, in general, a petty person.

There was simply something about Juliette, the Princess of Kensley Automobiles, that got to me.

In retrospect, I absolutely chose to see her through a very narrow scope. And through the eyes of someone who was looking for reasons to find fault in her.

Because, in my mind, I didn't think she understood the enormity of the legacy she was being handed on a silver platter. I didn't see her fawning over the plans for new models. I didn't feel she appreciated how mind-boggling a Kensley was to someone who knew anything at all about cars.

She was looking toward innovation without respecting that there was such a thing as perfection, things that required no significant changes.

A Kensley was pure perfection.

She couldn't—or didn't want to—see that.

And, to me, she seemed proud of that.

Which made me want to educate her.

When that failed—because she proved to be every bit as stubborn as I was—I seemed to set about to take her down a peg or two, knock her off that pedestal, make her see that she wasn't always right.

Things had been relatively tame then.

We didn't get along, but it wasn't pure animosity either.

Then she disappeared, ripping the rug out from under her father's feet, leaving him scrambling and unsure of himself.

After that, well, we couldn't seem to cross paths without it nearly turning into shouting matches.

Why, I wasn't sure.

I didn't have the best opinion of her after watching her father grieve her refusal to take the reins of his legacy. But she seemed to have undiluted derision toward me, the roots of which I didn't know.

We managed to fight over everything from carbon footprints to how good—or bad—the food was that was being served at whatever event we were attending at the same time.

It hadn't exactly escaped me, though, that it was just me.

Over the years, I'd never seen her arguing with anyone else.

It was something she saved for me.

When I'd even let it slip once how argumentative she was at a party, everyone around me furrowed their brows and said they often called her Sunshine because she was always so happy and easy-going.

Everyone you meet will have a different definition of you in their mind.

That was something Mitch had told me after a work meeting when someone had called him a selfish, money-grubbing, bull-headed asshole. Which was contrary to everything I knew the man to be.

In everyone else's mind, Jett was completely opposite to how she was in mine.

It did make me have to wonder if maybe it wasn't her. It was what I brought out of her.

I knew myself well enough to know I could be stubborn and a bit of an instigator. Especially when it was about something that meant a lot to me.

So anytime Jett criticized Mitch who absolutely *was*—as Jett had thought—a father figure to me—as well as mentor and good friend—I automatically got defensive, felt the need to protect him, never stopping to think that maybe it wasn't my place, perhaps they had their own issues.

And, apparently, they did.

I'd noticed, of course, that she didn't exactly look like her parents, but I had never looked like my mother

THERE BETTER BE PIE

either. Everyone was different. It never occurred to me that she wasn't biologically related to Mitch. In my mind, he treated her just as any father would treat their daughter. I was sure, too, that he absolutely saw her as his own.

The fact that she maybe didn't always feel that way—that she felt like an imposter in his world—definitely spoke of issues they needed to get on the table and resolve.

I needed to butt out, respect the fact that it wasn't my place to get involved.

"Trip," Mitch called as I walked through the house, freezing from my trek from the hot tub and up to the second floor.

"Everything alright, Mitch?"

"I will talk to Jett tomorrow. She needs to offer you a real apology."

"She did, Mitch," I told him. Because it was the truth. I might have been pissed at the time, busy trying to work through my grief, the pain that felt like someone was clawing something out of my chest, but there was no denying that she was shattered to have said something that may have hurt me, may have rubbed salt in open wounds. Her apology was genuine. And the subsequent punishment handed to her from both me and her father was over the top. "It's all good. Don't worry about it."

"You're sure?"

"I'm sure. She didn't mean anything by it. She just misspoke. It's not a big thing. We've talked."

And argued. Once again. But that didn't need to be public knowledge.

"If you're sure."

"I am. Actually, Mitch," I called, turning back.

"Yeah?"

"She's a good kid," I told him, watching his eyes go soft, the tension slip from his jaw. "Don't be hard on her about one mistake," I added, going into my room, making my way to my luggage to grab something dry.

She was, by all accounts of those who knew her, a good kid. A good woman. And if I got my head out of my

THERE BETTER BE PIE

ass for a minute, I would stop judging her through my life experiences.

Sure, I couldn't fathom turning your back on your family's business. Family *empire*. But I had never walked in her shoes, had the discussions with Mitch that she'd had, gotten my hopes up only to have them dashed because I didn't share the same mindset as him.

It couldn't have been easy to have a vision only to get it squashed.

It even made sense that, eventually, she had enough. Enough of the disappointment, enough of the expectations she felt she would never meet.

Of course she wanted to work at a job where she felt heard and valued, where her efforts were rewarded.

That was what she had done.

There was no reason to be down on her about it.

I might never understand why the hell she drove around in a piece of crap car living in a city her father said she didn't like, never touching her trust fund or taking money from her stocks, why she chose to live like she was an average middle-class person when she was anything but that, but I had to imagine that she had her reasons.

We all did.

Like maybe the hidden little one I didn't even want to admit to myself, not even when I knew it was the damn truth.

The other reason I liked poking at her, picking unnecessary fights with her.

Because she was sexy as hell when she was riled.

She was beautiful all the time.

She lit up when she was smiling.

She glowed when she was laughing.

But she was the sexiest thing I had ever seen when she was pissed off.

Her eyes burned, her face flushed, her mannerisms got more exaggerated, her voice got stronger, more confident.

It was hot.

I liked it.
I hated myself for liking it.
She was the boss's only child.
She was the very definition of off-limits.
But, yeah, I liked it.
I couldn't help myself whenever I ran into her.
Especially because she never gave me those laughs or that smile that she did with everyone else.
The fights were all she gave me.
I took them, gladly, all the while knowing I wasn't supposed to be as into them as I was, that I wasn't meant to walk away from them feeling light, satisfied, and turned on.
Yet there was no denying that was exactly what happened most of the time.
Even now, drained from a long day, a long couple of weeks, even, I could feel the pressure in my stomach, the precursor to the hard-on I so often got after an interaction with Jett.
It was going to be a long, long holiday weekend trying to convince everyone else—not the least of whom myself—that I was indifferent, or a bit annoyed, by Jett.
Instead of the actual truth.
I'd had a small thing for her since the first time I met her.
And it had only been growing since then.
I could try to hide it, disguise it, label it as something else by picking fights, by covering it all with a thick layer of annoyance, throw everyone off with the constant nitpicking and constant disagreements.
But the truth was always right there underneath it all.
I had a thing for the boss's daughter.
And nothing could ever, ever come of it.

CHAPTER FIVE

Juliette

There might have been an icepick stabbing me in each temple, and the kind of dryness inside that made my organs feel dehydrated. Still, nothing—not a thing— could dull the bubbling sensation in my chest I called excitement as I dragged myself out of bed, taking my tired body into the bathroom to drink cold water right out of the tap, showering the bromine from the hot tub off my skin and body, then making quick work of throwing myself together, knowing that I would eventually be heading back upstairs to get dressed for dinner anyway.

Then I made my way down the stairs, already smelling the coffee when my feet met the top stair. By the time I was at the bottom, the music hit my ears, bringing a slow smile to my face, big enough to wipe away any lingering tiredness and pain.

"Cat Stevens?"

Not even Trip's voice could sour my mood on my favorite day of the year.

No.

In fact, I went ahead and shared that smile with him too.

THERE BETTER BE PIE

What can I say, I was a firm believer in setting aside differences for special days. Thanksgiving, for me, was a special day.

"It's my mom's baking music," I told him, finding him a little bleary-eyed, slow blinking at me as he put his arms through the holes of a big red sweatshirt, his hair still charmingly mussed from sleep. "Ever since I could remember, if I heard *Wild World* or *If You Want to Sing Out* playing, I knew she was making something sweet for us."

"You get started baking this early?" he asked, brows lowering, not seeming able to grasp the concept.

"Yeah. We have a lot to get done. You're in for a treat," I added, almost a little envious of being able to experience our Thanksgiving spread for the first time. It was special to me—someone who had known it since she was a baby—so I couldn't imagine how great it would be for someone who had never celebrated a traditional home-cooked Thanksgiving meal.

"I think you're right," he agreed, nodding.

"Why are you up so early?"

To that, he gave me what I could only call a sheepish smile. "I figure I need to work up an appetite for this," he told me.

"You're going for a run? It's freezing out."

"Worried I'm gonna catch frostbite?" he asked, eyes bright.

"I mean... there would be less of you to constantly be annoyed with if you lost a couple toes or fingertips..."

It wasn't meant as bait, and—for once—he didn't take it as such.

He just let out a chuckle, falling into step beside me. "Save some coffee for me, alright?" he asked, swerving off toward the back deck while I moved forward into the kitchen.

"Was that Trip I just heard?" my mother asked from the other side of the island where she already had dough nestled on a bed of fluffy flour, her giant rolling pin in her delicate hand.

THERE BETTER BE PIE

"Yeah. He's going for a run. He needs to watch his figure," I added, going toward the coffee machine, knowing it was going to be a long day if I didn't start loading up early.

"I think that is the first time I've seen you talk about him without a big scowl on," she said. As I turned my head over my shoulder, I found her shooting me an odd, almost suggestive smile.

"What?" I asked, confused, not sure how to interpret her look.

"Oh, nothing," she said, still smiling as she started rolling.

"No," I countered, turning fully. "Not nothing. What?"

"I just happened to come out last night to grab some tea before bed. I saw the two of you in the hot tub. You were smiling at each other."

"Oh, my God. You don't think something is happening between us, do you?" I asked, snorting.

"Crazier things have happened."

"Have they, though?" I asked, going to grab some creamer for my coffee. "We can't stand each other."

"You know that old saying about there being a fine line between love and hate?"

"Oh, that old, outdated cliche?" I shot back, rolling my eyes. "There is a giant cavern between love and hate. There is a *Grand Canyon* between it."

"Oh, to be young and know everything," she shot back, swiping her hair out of her face, leaving a trail of whiteness on her cheekbone. "Cliches are cliches because they were true so often that it became annoying, and people needed to slap a title on it."

"I don't love Trip, Mom," I clarified, tone a little apologetic since she clearly had her heart set on it a little bit.

"I didn't say you loved him, honey. I said that you two—for a short while—were happy in each other's presence. And I *implied* that all that snapping you two do together requires a lot of passion."

"Passion. That is a new way to describe pure derision."

"Sweetheart, if you truly abhorred someone, you wouldn't bother wasting your time arguing with them."

Well damn.

She wasn't exactly wrong about that, was she?

There were plenty of people I had come across in my life that I had no use for, that I would never waste my energy on, that I knew were best just avoided rather than spending precious breath on them.

"Just a thought," she added, waving the topic away, but I didn't miss the spark in her eyes before her gaze dipped once again.

"What are you working on?" I asked, wanting desperately to occupy my mind with any thought other than a possibility of her being—even a small bit—correct about Trip and me.

"Pecan pie," she told me, smile warm. Because it was my father's favorite, because she loved making it for him.

It wasn't the first time I was really hit with the impact of their affection for each other. It was hard to be around them without being acutely aware of it. The stolen touches, the lingering glances, the way that—even when across a room—when one of them laughed, the other turned and smiled.

They were the real deal.

The hard-won happily-ever-after everyone dreams of.

Something about it felt different for me right that moment, though.

Maybe it was just getting older, maturing, seeing the world through a different light.

But I wasn't sure I had ever been aware of how much I wanted what they had until that moment.

THERE BETTER BE PIE

Most of my life had been spent trying to prove myself, to show everyone that I was my own person, that I was more than a blue blood, that I had my own worth, my own path, my own ambitions.

It wasn't easy to make a name for yourself, to disassociate from the way everyone saw you, thought of you.

But, well, I was pretty sure I had finally accomplished that. My job was stable. My accounts were plump and happy. I was just a few years away from my ultimate dream.

There had never been space in my life for anything other than me and my ambitions.

Now, though, I was starting to see there was room. Not only that, but I wanted someone to fill that space, to look at me the way my father looked at my mother even after all these years. I wanted to smile down at my pie crust because I was picturing the joy my husband would feel at consuming it.

Those were worthwhile ambitions, just as fulfilling as my career ones.

"Honey, what are you going to start with?" she asked, snapping me out of my musings, making me jerk hard enough to spill my coffee on my hands.

"Oh, um... I guess apple. And then pumpkin." Those were my true specialties, where I shined.

My mother always had the pecan, and blueberry and cherry was where my mother excelled.

We got lost in our routine, both wholly confident in our practiced motions, humming along with the music, chatting here and there, but mostly lost in the process, content in our silence.

It was about an hour later when a red splash of color moved in my peripheral, making me jolt a little when it was beside me in a moment, smelling woodsy.

"Whatcha making?" he asked, reaching with one hand for the coffee carafe.

"Oh, ah, apple pie. These are the spices," I added lamely, seeing as I was literally shaking cinnamon into a bowl.

"How many pies are there going to be?" he asked, leaning against the island at my side. Close. Distractingly close. I lost count of the shakes of cinnamon. I was never a woman for spoons when it came to baking. My mother was the same way. *You measure with your heart.*

"Oh, usually at least five."

"*Five*?" he asked, eyes bulging a bit.

"We're going to spoil you for anyone else," I agreed, nodding. "Now, any table that serves less than five pies is going to be a bitter disappointment."

"I can think of worse things than being spoiled by pies," he told me, reaching out with curious fingers toward the bowl of slices, earning a slap that cracked through the mostly quiet space.

"Everything needs a taste test," he told me.

"Not my apple pie. My apple pie is perfect."

"I dunno... the one I used to get at the diner was pretty good."

"Now you're insulting me," I told him, but I was smiling while I did so.

"I'll be right back, kids," my mother cheered, voice a bit too pleased, rushing off with a smile of her own.

"You're happy this morning," Trip observed when we were alone. "I thought you'd have a killer hangover with all that wine."

"I did. Do," I clarified, still feeling wrung dry and a little wobbly in the belly, reminding me that I needed to eat something to soak up what was left of the alcohol in my stomach. "But not even that can spoil today for me."

"That's a good mindset," he agreed, watching me a bit too intensely, making me shuffle my feet. "Easy," he said when his hand reached out, thumb tracing unexpectedly down my jaw, sending a shiver through my belly—and something decidedly less tame through *another* area of my

THERE BETTER BE PIE

anatomy. "You had some flour on your jaw," he added, eyes holding mine.

"Oh, ah, thanks," I mumbled, finding it impossible to pull my gaze from his, despite knowing this level of eye-contact either meant we wanted to screw—or kill—each other.

"Oh, good," my father's voice boomed, accompanied by a loud clap and hand-rubbing he was always known for. "You guys are getting along. Trip, you ready to hunker down on the couch and be waited on hand and foot?" he asked, doing so just because he knew he'd get a reaction out of me.

"Yep. Trip, this is amazing. It is the one day out of the year where we are all magically transported back to the 1950s, where all the womenfolk are good for is beer refills and dinner making. In high heels and a full face of makeup."

"Just the one day, huh?"

"All other three-hundred-sixty-four days, you have to get your own damn beer refills," I informed him.

"Oh, your mother is making my favorite," my father declared, glancing in the oven. He sounded surprised. He always did. Despite getting the same thing every single Thanksgiving since they'd gotten together. "Looks like you hit the trails this morning, huh, Trip? After your shower, come meet me in the living room. We gotta watch the parade. It's tradition," he added, moving off in said direction.

"What?" I asked, finding Trip's gaze a little far away, almost a little confused-looking.

"Nothing. It's just... this is nice," he said, shaking his head, knocking some pesky, clinging thoughts loose.

"It is," I agreed, nodding, finding—for the first time—that it was no *less* nice for his presence. And, maybe, it was even enhanced by it. You know, when we weren't at each other's throats, that is.

"Was your father in here poking around?" my mother asked, reemerging, her hair pulled back, knowing we were getting closer to the more serious part of the day—the preparations for the meal itself.

"Always," I agreed as Trip pushed away from the island, away from me, though still fiddling around behind me for a few minutes. I had no idea what he was doing until I saw a plate slide in at my side with two slices of wheat toast spread with butter and raspberry jam.

He'd made me toast.

He'd made me toast.

And then just kept walking like it was nothing. Like he did it all the time. Like we hadn't been yelling at each other just hours before.

"It doesn't mean anything," I told my mother whose lips were twitching as I reached for a slice, looking forward to an end of the wobbling sensation in my belly.

"No, no. Of course it doesn't, dear."

Even as she said it, though, I knew we both thought differently.

It *did* mean something.

I then spent the next few hours trying to convince myself that all it meant was he was putting down a white flag, that we were calling a truce, that we both decided we were done snapping at each other. At least for the day.

Because anything other than that, well, that would be completely ridiculous, right?

CHAPTER SIX

Trip

I missed my mother so much it was almost hard to breathe.

Her absence was a weight pressing on my chest, stealing my air.

Invariably, we would be sitting on the couch together watching the parade. She'd be singing along to all the songs that I never knew, grinning huge at the marching bands, regaling me with stories of her marching band days, about how it was always every kid's dream to make it to the Macy's Thanksgiving Day Parade.

We'd watch Santa come while wondering aloud if the pie at the diner would be as good as it had been the year before, if the chef would be the same, if the recipe had changed.

She loved the pumpkin.

I loved the apple.

I would still get pie.

I still got the parade.

But I didn't get my mom.

I would never get my mom again.

It was a harsh reality, one I was still—at times—struggling to wrap my head around.

THERE BETTER BE PIE

And it made me feel guilty, in a way, at finding a small bit of comfort, of joy in this new experience.

I knew she wouldn't have wanted me to sit around and mourn, to be alone on a family holiday. It would have broken her heart to think of that as my reality.

It still, in a small way, felt disloyal, though, to sit with Mitch and watch the parade, to hear him talk about the meal to come.

There was no denying, though, that there was comfort in the whole thing, in being a part of a family, even if I was only invited out of a bit of pity.

"You stole my spot," Jett accused, trying to nudge me out of the corner with the tip of her sock-covered foot.

"I was here first," I reminded her, refusing to budge. Maybe because I knew she couldn't see the TV from her angle, which meant she had to move closer, almost her entire body pressing up to my side.

"Yeah, but this is my spot. Historically. It has the perfect view of the TV and is just far enough away from my parents that I don't have to hear them talk about the wind and the balloons for the twenty-ninth year in a row."

"How's the hangover?" I asked, watching as she sipped her coffee, cradling the cup with both hands as she pulled her knees in toward her chest.

"Gone. I knew my body wouldn't let it hang around. Not on Thanksgiving, of all days."

I had to admit, Thanksgiving had never been my favorite of holidays. It always felt a little, I don't know, in the way. Wedged right between Halloween and Christmas, it always lacked a little of the oomph that both the holidays surrounding it had.

Seeing it through Jett's eyes, though, was starting to make me appreciate it in a way I maybe never would have on my own.

Sure, she liked the whole no-presents-required thing because she was, apparently, a terrible gift-giver, but I never stopped to consider how refreshing it was that a holiday existed without that expectation. Sure, an argument could be

THERE BETTER BE PIE

made for New Years or Fourth of July, but those had never really been holidays I celebrated. I always passed out before the ball dropped. And ever since I started at Kensley, I had been going to *their* Independence Day celebrations.

Thanksgiving was the only family holiday that I partook in that required no gifts.

All the others—Christmas, Easter, Valentine's day—required at least something small. Halloween required little gifts in the form of cheap chocolate given to dozens or hundreds of people.

Thanksgiving was simply a day for togetherness and food and the gratefulness that you could have both of those things.

It was refreshing.

And I found myself looking at it in a whole new way.

"Tired from all the cooking yet?"

"Oh, my God. We've barely even started," she told me, shaking her head like I was out of my mind.

"You've been working in there for hours already."

"All the desserts. And we've been prepping."

"Prepping," I repeated, watching as her gaze moved to me when the TV cut to commercial.

"Cutting up the potatoes, making the salad, getting all the veggies washed. The actual cooking is going to start after Santa comes and lets us know the gift-giving season is upon us."

"What's the worst gift you've ever given someone?" I asked, not quite able to believe she was as bad at it as she claimed.

"I gave my boss tickets to the opera two years back."

"That seems like a thoughtful gift."

"She's tone-deaf. Literally. Music means very little to her. Something I didn't remember until after she opened the box and gave me a very forced smile."

"Alright. That is pretty bad," I agreed, chuckling.

"I swear my mind just like... turns off when I am in a store—or online—trying to find something for someone."

"But you buy for the kids at the shelter."

"Yeah, well, kids are easy. If it squishes or talks or sings or lights or vomits glitter everywhere, they are over the moon."

"You like kids?" I asked, trying to remind myself that it was a stupid question to ask, that there was no reason I would need to know the answer to it.

"The kids at the shelter are amazing. So sweet and adaptive. I mean... no one should have to celebrate Christmas in a shelter, but their eyes still light up, they still squeal and laugh and hold up their favorite gifts over their heads with giant smiles so their moms can snap pictures."

"You want kids?"

"If my kids can be half as sweet as those ones are, yeah. And, don't," she demanded, shooting me a raised brow.

"Don't what?"

"Don't say that any child of mine would probably be argumentative and stubborn and—what else have you accused me of being?"

"I wasn't going to say any of that," I assured her. I wasn't, either. In fact, while she talked about kids, my mind went to a couple little round-faced kids with her honey eyes and a big smile holding up their favorite gifts.

"Well... good," she said, lost for anything else to say since she'd likely been waiting for a fight.

Quite frankly, though, I was happy to be done fighting. Having a bit of a truce between us was nice. As much as I did think she was hot when she was angry, I was finding that I liked this too. The common ground, the growing familiarity.

It was nice in its own way.

Comfortable, even.

Suddenly, it felt like I belonged, not just like I was a stranger infringing upon their hospitality, taking advantage of their pity.

THERE BETTER BE PIE

"Starting to smell good," I mumbled, taking a deep breath of the cooking turkey, a scent that had been wafting through the house for about an hour already.

"Just wait. Mashed potatoes, stuffing, rolls. You're going to be glad you didn't eat anything even if you are starving right now."

"What's your favorite part of the meal?"

"The stuffing. It took us years to perfect the recipe, but it is amazing. My mom's mashed potatoes are a real hit, though. She keeps the skin on and has the exact right ratio of flavors. You're never going to want to eat anywhere else again."

"I'm looking forward to it. I've always been a mashed potato kind of guy."

"People who don't love mashed potatoes are just not my kind of people," she declared with a shrug. "Oh, here comes Santa," she said, eyes bright, smile spreading.

I didn't watch Santa.

I watched Jett watching Santa, finding something unexpectedly pure in her face, something raw and real and open-- a little glimpse into her soul, maybe. "Oh, good. He's normal Santa."

"Normal Santa?" I repeated, glancing at the TV to see your typical Santa stand-in.

"I was half-worried they'd give him a makeover, put him on a keto diet or something. The world isn't ready for Sexy Santa. We like the jolly, rotund dude who we can bribe with cookies and milk."

Jett could sometimes be touchy about weight subjects. And her mother constantly calling her Pudge likely didn't help, even if I knew Kathy well enough to know she meant absolutely nothing by it. Like when an owner of a dog called it a Big Dummy affectionately.

It seemed like a part of Jett, though, still saw herself as the girl she had been years before, still stuck in that spiral of insecurity. Even though she had nothing to feel unsure about.

She was gorgeous, almost painful to look at sometimes, knowing you couldn't touch, but wanting nothing more than to reach out.

Alright.

No.

That was enough of those kinds of thoughts.

Her parents were sitting a few feet away from me, for chrissakes.

Besides, I was only torturing myself.

She was off-limits.

Even if she wasn't, the woman could barely tolerate me on a good day.

There was never going to be anything between us.

"Alright. Time to get to work," Jett declared, slamming a hand down on my knee so she could haul herself onto her feet. "Don't fill up on too much beer," she admonished before practically skipping away, followed by an equally excited Kathy.

"You two seem to be getting on much better," Mitch observed when we were once again alone, hand already reaching for the remote, looking for the game that would be on in a few.

"We have come to a bit of an understanding," I told him.

"What kind of understanding is that?"

"That we're both relatively pleasant people to everyone but each other. And if we aren't looking for reasons to snipe at each other, that we get along alright."

"It always surprised me that you two never got on. I've never met anyone who didn't love Jett. And you've always been popular with everyone at the plant."

"I think it may have more to do with a core misunderstanding about our places in your life, in your family business," I told him, wondering how much was too much to say, what was her story to tell.

"I guess that makes sense. You stepped into the place she vacated."

"Exactly," I agreed, wanting to let it drop, understanding that Jett would only find peace if she were the one confronting her dad with her issues.

"She's coming back."

"What?" I asked, jolting a bit at the shock.

"Not for your job, of course," he clarified, sending me a smirk.

"For what job then?"

"Jett is a little proud. When she went off to college, I think she saw herself through the eyes of people who were prejudiced against people with large amounts of wealth. It screwed with her head. that's why she sold her car, why she doesn't touch the money that is rightfully hers. She felt like she needed to prove herself, make a name for herself. One that had nothing to do with Kensley Automobiles. And, honestly, with a little distance from the whole thing, I can understand that. But she will be coming back."

"How do you know that?"

"She doesn't tell me a lot about her plans. But she tells Kath. And Kath talks to me. Jett only plans to be in the city a few more years at the most. She misses a small-town community. She wants a house, not an apartment. She wants to be close to us again. I figure she will use some of her trust or her savings to buy herself a house. That will keep her busy for a while. Fixing it up with her mom. But I know my girl. She's gonna get bored. she's going to need an outlet for it."

"So you think she'd come back to Kensley?" I asked, not seeing it myself.

"In a different capacity. I think she is going to eventually approach me about the fact that we have no social media, that if we want to appeal to this new class of millionaires coming up, we need to be accessible in a way that is familiar to them."

And she would be able to pull that off.

With her social media 'fiddling.'

Actually, I could see that.

THERE BETTER BE PIE

Because it was clear that Kensley did mean something to her. Even if she didn't have the right vision for how to create new cars for the future, she did have the knowhow to make sure the company would stay relevant.

She would get to be a part of the family legacy without having to battle with her father over ideas.

"It's part of the reason I always secretly hoped you two would get over your issues. One day, I am going to take a step back. It would give me peace of mind to know that the people I'd like to leave in charge can stop yelling at each other for long enough to run the company."

Run the company?

I knew Mitch liked me. I knew that he was comfortable with me taking more of a leadership role. But it never would have crossed my mind that he expected me to co-run his family business with his daughter. I never would have even allowed myself to hope for such a thing.

"Yeah, you heard me right," he agreed, taking in the shock that had to have been plastered on my face. "I want you two to take over someday. As a team. So this holiday, it is giving me hope that this would be a possibility in the future. You know, if you want that kind of responsibility," he added, looking a bit unsure. A man like Mitch Kensley did not look unsure often. Which meant that my answer was clearly important to him.

While I never could have expected him to leave so much in my hands, there was no denying that it was like my childhood dreams come to life. Kensley Autos *was* my life. And now, apparently, my future, my legacy.

That, well, that meant everything to me.

"I would be honored to have that responsibility," I told him, and no one could doubt the sincerity in my tone.

"Good. When the time comes, we will talk about it. But Kathy would not be happy to hear us talking business on a holiday. So, for now, we will watch the game."

Watch the game we did as the sounds of chopping and chattering came from the kitchen.

THERE BETTER BE PIE

At some point—and I wasn't even fully aware of doing this—I shifted my position on the couch, giving me a much worse view of the TV, but a much better view of the kitchen. And, more specifically, Jett.

Unaware of any eyes on her, she alternated between smiling and laughing with her mother to leaning over whatever task she was doing, brows a little furrowed, hips swaying along to music which seemed to shift away from Cat Stevens and toward what seemed to be Christmas carols.

"Need a refill?" I asked Mitch, jerking my chin toward his dead soldier, looking for an excuse to make my way into the kitchen, to be a small part of the goings-on.

"That'd be great. See if you could sneak some food, too. I'm starving."

"I'll see what I can do," I told him, having to remind myself to keep my steps calm and casual as I made my way into the kitchen, happening to walk up behind Jett, looking over her shoulder.

"What are you making?"

"Jesus, you scared me," she said, her knife flying out of her hand.

"Maybe you'd have heard me if you weren't belting out *Let It Snow*," I told her, nudging her hip with mine as I moved in toward her side. She sang atrociously off-key too. Which was unexpectedly charming.

"Oh, Jetty loves snow. She used to go to sleep *every* night in elementary school with her pajamas inside out, hoping it would make it snow. Even in the summer," Kathy added, smiling.

"I was an optimistic kid. Or I was in the know about some prescient insight about upcoming global warming as I grew up."

"Do you like snow, Trip?"

"I like it when I don't have to drive to work in it," I told her.

THERE BETTER BE PIE

"Mitch didn't send you in here on some covert mission to steal food, did he?" Kathy asked, clearly knowing her husband too well.

"I offered a beer. But he might have suggested a little thievery."

"Mom stopped baking pies ahead of time because she would wake up on Thanksgiving morning to find he'd taken slices out of each of them."

"Well, if they are as good as you claim, can you blame him?"

"Do you hear that, Ma? He doubts our baking ability."

"Well," Kathy said, clucking her tongue, "We will just have to show him, won't we?"

"One of the few times I will be happy to be proven wrong. Seriously, what are you making?" I asked as she grabbed her knife again, slicing the top off what seemed to be some kind of squash.

"Oh, another of Jetty's traditions. She makes us pumpkin soup served in squash bowls."

"You serve soup in a hollowed-out squash?" I asked, a bit overwhelmed by the pageantry of it all. "For family?"

"It's nice to be able to go over-the-top," Jett explained. "Even if no one sees it but us."

"We know you must be starving, Trip. It's going to be another two hours, give or take. If you want to sneak a little snack, we won't hold it against you."

Jett's raised brow said otherwise.

"I think I am going to wait it out. You guys aren't slaving away so I come to the table too full to enjoy it all."

The smile that spread across Jett's face let me know I said the right thing.

And I was kicking myself for taking too much pride in that.

I grabbed the beers, resisting the urge to sneak a piece of the cornbread that was set to cool on the counter.

Moving past Jett, I leaned over her shoulder one more time, seeing all four of the squash lined up, ready to be filled.

"Looks good, Princess," I said, lips close to her ear so that only she could hear.

The problem was, it was close enough that I felt the shiver that moved through her at the sound of my voice.

Christ.

Sure, I had been dealing with my attraction toward her since I had met her, but I had never once stopped to wonder if she felt anything even remotely similar for me.

Because she outwardly seemed to despise me.

That said, any outsider would think I felt the same way toward her. Even if, underneath it all, I was hiding a pretty fierce attraction.

Was it possible that Jett did as well?

Had the thought even crossed my mind the day before, I would have scoffed.

But that shiver...

That had nothing to do with being cold. She had her sleeves rolled up, had a barely noticeable bead of sweat in her brows. She was hot.

Yet she shivered.

Because of me.

Because of my closeness.

Because of my breath on her ear.

Sure, an argument could be made for it being an involuntary thing.

I just wasn't inclined to buy into that.

Not given our history, not given the passion with which she fought with me.

Maybe, all long, she had been fostering something other than blind hatred toward me as well. Even if she wasn't fully aware of it. Even if she would never even admit it to herself.

Some things were chemical.

You couldn't control it.

THERE BETTER BE PIE

I dropped down on the couch, cracking open the beer she had picked out— always impeccably chosen by Jett even though she couldn't drink it herself—and tried to remind myself that her being attracted to me didn't change anything.

She was still off-limits.

She was still the daughter of the boss.

She was still someone I could never lay a hand on. No matter how hard it was getting to control that urge.

I sat there staring at the TV, not really seeing any of it, until Kathy suddenly appeared, eyes a little tired, but smile warm.

"We are close to serving," she informed us. There was something suggested in her voice, something I didn't know her well enough to place.

"She means it is time for us to break out those suits I told you we needed to pack," Mitch translated, making me immediately hop up to do so.

I wasn't much for suits. I rarely had cause to wear one. That just wasn't the life I led. I didn't run in suit-wearing circles.

I actually had to buy one just for this occasion because my old one was a piece of crap cheap black thing I got on a sale years before when I had needed it for a funeral.

"I'll be right back down," I told Kathy who was pulling off her apron, likely off to change too.

I noticed as I passed that Jett was gone. When I got in my room, stripping out of my clothes, I could hear the footsteps of her in the room above, moving around, likely removing her clothes as well.

It took actual work not to picture her up there doing so, forcing myself to focus on what I was doing instead, getting myself together.

By the time I heard the click of her heels on the stairs, I was finished with the damn tie that had evaded me for a while.

I rushed out of the room, finding myself curious to see her all dressed up.

I'd seen her in various outfits over the years. She always had a good sense of style, looking put together in anything she wore. But I had never seen her dressed formally. Mitch was not a formal kind of guy, so none of the work events required any sort of dress code.

I just rounded the corner when she stepped onto the landing on my floor.

"Wow."

It was out of me before I could stop it. A knee-jerk, honest reaction. That alerted her to my presence, making her jolt and turn fully, giving me an even better view.

The dress skimmed her curves and skirted the floor in a deep red wine color, the V of the bodice low enough to show the barest hint of cleavage, forcing you to want to pull it wider, see what she was hiding underneath. The material itself looked buttery smooth, begged to be touched.

If all that wasn't bad enough, when she moved, I was made acutely aware of the slit that slid up her thigh, exposing the very top of her thigh above her knee.

Another place to spread the material, spread *her*, get a taste.

Damnit.

I needed to think of literally anything other than that.

"I've never seen you in a suit," she said, voice as soft as her eyes seemed to be as they moved over me.

"I've never seen you in a dress like that," I responded, letting my eyes do one more once-over, trying to convince myself that once would give me my fill. When I knew that the only sight better than her *in* that dress would be her *out* of that dress.

"It's new," she said, self-consciously running a hand down her belly then off her thigh when she caught what she was doing.

"You should wear it daily."

To that, her smile spread, until it was beaming. "I think it might be a tad too dressy for work and running errands."

"Everyone should see you in that dress."

"Are you drunk?" she asked, the smile wobbling a bit.

"What? No. Why?"

"You're being weirdly nice to me," she said, gathering her hair, pulling it to one side of her neck, the motion showing her back as she turned toward the stairs again.

"Wait," I said, moving in behind her, hands reaching out, grabbing both ends of the top of her dress that she hadn't zipped.

"Oh, I was going to have my mom do it for me. I tried for an embarrassingly long minute to try to get it."

"I got it," I assured her, feeling the heat of her skin against my fingertips as I grabbed the zipper, slowly pulling it up. So slowly that it would almost be comical, but in that moment, it felt right, felt necessary, to take my time with it, to be close to her when she would let me.

But too soon it was over and we needed to go down. We could both see Kathy moving around the kitchen in her heels and ice blue dress.

"Here," I said, offering her my arm as she debated her ability to get down the stairs in heels with a dress easily tripped upon.

Her gaze moved over me once again before her hand gathered a bit of her skirt in her other hand as she laced her arm through mine.

"You ready to eat?"

"I'm a little light-headed," I admitted. I could normally go a while without eating with no issue, but the run—which, admittedly, I had gone so hard on because I was trying to work through some of my sexual frustration—had me hungrier than usual.

"Well, it's a good thing that we are about to feed you then."

"Oh, don't you two make a beautiful picture?" her mother exclaimed as we finally hit the bottom landing. She didn't immediately release me, and I was certainly not going

THERE BETTER BE PIE

to pull away first. "Trip, would you mind handling the turkey? I already have Mitch on pouring the drinks."

Without a choice, I slid my arm from Jett's, moving across the room to help her mother.

From there, it was a blur of their bodies moving in and out of the kitchen until the table was set, all the while waving us away when we tried to get up to help.

It was an enormous table. But every square inch of it was covered in an almost obscene number of dishes.

Turkey, fluffy mashed potatoes, a giant bowl of stuffing, corn, broccoli, honey glazed roasted whole rainbow carrots, roasted Brussels sprouts, baked macaroni and cheese, green bean casserole, golden cornbread, puffy biscuits, boats of gravy, bowls of cranberry sauce that didn't come from a can. And, of course, the soup in squash bowls sitting directly on our plates that were trimmed in autumnal plaid colors.

It was insane.

In the most amazing way possible.

"Alrighty, well," Mitch said, breaking the silence as we all seemed a bit overwhelmed by the spread before us. "We don't usually do Grace, but we do tend to go around the table and list something we are thankful for this year."

That, at least, was something familiar to me. My mother and I had a similar tradition. Even in the lean years. She believed it was important, no matter how bad things were, to be grateful for something. And so we always had to each come up with three things.

Some years, it was for basic things many took for granted. We were thankful for heat, for light, for food in our bellies. Other years, fuller years, we were thankful for more superficial things.

"Trip, you're the guest," Mitch went on. "Would you like to lead us off?"

"That's an easy one. This year, I am thankful to have been invited to celebrate with your family on a holiday that would have otherwise been very depressing."

THERE BETTER BE PIE

"We are so happy to have you," Kathy said, reaching over to place her hand over mine, giving it an affectionate squeeze. "I am grateful for your presence at our table."

"I am thankful that you and Jetty worked out your differences," Mitch added, and I knew he meant that from a deeper level, one surrounded by his dreams for the future.

"Pudge?" Kathy prompted.

Jett's lips curved up at one side, mischief dancing in her eyes as her gaze slid to me. "I am grateful for the opportunity to prove to Trip that my pie will always be far superior to diner pie."

With that, well, we dug in.

And it was like nothing I had ever experienced before, like I knew I would never experience again unless I was invited back to this table.

I couldn't even fit a small portion of everything on my plate at once, but I somehow managed to sock away seconds of mashed potatoes and stuffing before my stomach absolutely refused to stretch to fit anything else.

Around me, everyone else seemed to be suffering the same predicament, leaning back in their chairs, hands pressing to stomachs.

"Someone is going to need to roll me to the living room," Jett announced, drawing a chuckle from her parents.

"How are we supposed to fit pie in after this?" I asked, yanking at the tie that was starting to irritate me.

"Time," Jett informed me. "That's why we eat so early. Then we can relax for a few hours, then come back for seconds or dessert. Mom and Dad usually go take a walk if you want to join them."

"You don't?"

"That would involve *walking*, and as we have already established, I am only capable of rolling at the moment."

"Kathy, why don't you and Mitch take your walk? I will put all this away," I offered.

THERE BETTER BE PIE

"Don't be a hero, Trip," Jett told me. "We usually just leave it for a bit, and come back to clean up later. I know the couch is beckoning you."

I won't lie, it was. Nothing sounded less fun than gathering up the food, finding containers, and playing Tetris with the refrigerator contents.

With that, we broke off in our separate directions. Mitch and Kathy gathered their coats, taking off out the back door.

Jett kicked out of her heels and made slow progress toward the living room, dropping down into her spot.

I, not wanting the temptation of her sprawled out on the couch in that dress, took myself into the kitchen to put on a pot of coffee, washing a couple of the pots I thought wouldn't fit in the dishwasher, trying to keep my body—and mind—occupied until Mitch and Kathy came back, ripping away any temptation I absolutely was harboring to go into that living room, grab that woman, and take her back to my room.

"Alright, who is ready for pie?" Kathy declared about an hour and a half later, after we had all pitched in and gotten the leftovers put away. It was enough to feed an army, but I found myself excited at the prospect of Thanksgiving leftovers, another luxury I had never experienced before.

"Ready to be proven wrong, Trip?" Jett asked, making me turn to find her standing there in her bare feet, still in *that* dress, a pie in each hand, waving them around at me.

I didn't care if the pies tasted like friggen dirt.

I was going to tell her they were the best things I have ever tasted.

As it turned out, I wouldn't have to lie.

I was never so happy to be wrong.

Because Jett's smile lit up the damn room.

CHAPTER SEVEN

Jett

After dinner was always a tryptophan-induced blur.

The entire day rushed me at once, sapping me of whatever seemingly bottomless well of energy there had been that had gotten me up at the crack of dawn, and happily working for several long hours slaving away at a grand meal.

I felt wrung out, dead tired, and, well, there was no nice way of putting this, fat. And not in that metaphorical, my-self-worth-has-too-much-to-do-with-the-scale kind of way. In a very literal kind of way.

Even I would admit that my dress looked hot as hell when I had put it on, but there was no doubt that I was currently looking about four months pregnant.

I mean... my *underwear* band was tight.

All I had on my mind as I made the slow climb up two flights of stairs was wiping off my makeup, sliding off my dress, then dropping into bed.

But then I had to go and catch sight of Trip as he made his way up the stairs toward his room, his tie already pulled loose, his hands steadily yanking his shirt out of his pants, exposing a delicious sliver of belly before he ducked into his room and out of sight.

Delicious.

"Oh, God," I grumbled, pressing my forehead against my bedroom door.

I wanted to deny it, of course.

I wanted to hide from something that was becoming more and more true as the hours pressed on.

I was attracted to Trip.

Maybe that wouldn't be a revelation to most people. He was a good-looking man with a good job and the kind of smile that felt like the sun was beaming down on you, making you want to lean into it, get more of that warmth.

But to me, yeah, it was a big deal.

Because, well, maybe my mother was right after all. Maybe the line between love and hate was not as defined as I wanted to believe. Maybe the line was only there because I had drawn it there myself, used it as an excuse to push down or deny the truth.

I was a little bit into Trip Martin.

Once the issues were all laid out on the table, examined, dissected, making us both see what they truly were on closer inspection, which was nothing like what we had originally thought from a distance, well, it became impossible to call this anything other than what it was.

A long-buried, heavily denied attraction.

Sure, I wasn't determined to hate the man anymore. I was beginning to grasp that my issues with him really stemmed from a deeper issue within myself, something that had nothing to do with him, and that I had only used him as a scapegoat because it was easier than to attempt to seek out my own healing.

Beyond that, maybe we rubbed each other the wrong way because we were looking for excuses not to like each other. Because we both knew that nothing could happen between us.

God, my father would have a conniption if he thought Trip and I had something going on.

His only daughter.
And the-son-he-never-had.
No.
Nothing could ever happen.
Of course not.
But there was no denying that there was want there.
I wanted.

I needed, at first, to believe my eye-banging him in the hot tub was simply the alcohol and the intimacy of half-nudity and warm water, that I was just hard up, that he was red-blooded male and I was a red-blooded woman whose sex drive had not been sated in far too long.

There was no denying, though, that it was more than that, that it was maybe even a little deeper than that.

See, when we stopped snapping at each other, I finally got to see what everyone else saw in Trip.

That he was a good man. That he was charming and light-hearted, that he went with the flow, that he was happy to lend a hand, that he was quick with a compliment and a laugh.

It was no wonder my father was so fond of him.
I mean... he'd made me toast.
He complimented my squash bowls.
And then, well, he'd liked me in my dress.
More than I liked him in a suit.
Which was saying something.
Because I really, really liked him in a suit.

But his eyes had glided over me with scorching heat; I was almost surprised the material didn't singe as he looked at me.

Every inch of my skin certainly felt hot in their wake.

Which was nothing compared to the inferno of need that grasped my system at the hunger I saw in his eyes.

Then, oh, then.
Then he touched me.
It was chaste.
I'd had men zip me up plenty of times.

THERE BETTER BE PIE

It never felt like *foreplay* before.

But his fingers moved like a shiver over my skin. Then that shiver went ahead and moved through my insides too, pooling into need at the juncture of my thighs.

As if all of that wasn't enough, he had to go ahead and be a gentleman, offering me his arm, leading me down the stairs, helping serve and clean up after dinner.

That's the whole package, my mother would say with an approving nod.

And, well, it was, wasn't it?

Someone who worked hard and took care of himself, who was dedicated to his job, loyal to those he cared about, charming, kind, generous, gentlemanly, and, well, hot.

Add in the fact that he managed to stoke a passion in me like never before—even if that passion had previously been in a negative way—then, yeah, it was everything.

He had everything to offer.

On top of all of that, my parents loved him.

Which was a pretty big deal.

I hadn't exactly been the best at picking partners in the past.

There was Richard Heinsburg, the Fifth. Who was rich enough that he thought he could get away with mild kleptomania. Until he stole my great grandmother's brooch.

Then there were my college flames. River, the slam poet who thought that handing out fliers for a vegan fast food place could be considered a career for the rest of his life. And Heath, the soulful singer-songwriter who wrote love songs for me. And then for the six other girls I found out he had been dating at the same time.

In my older adulthood, there was another underachiever, an over-achiever who liked his job more than me, and my most recent ex. Jaxson who didn't believe in labels or reproduction or—evidently—paying his taxes.

It sort of said something that your easiest breakup involved tax evasion, the police, and imprisonment.

THERE BETTER BE PIE

To say my parents were less than thrilled about all these 'missteps of the heart,' as my mother would put it, was an understatement.

I had started to think I was doomed in the love department. That it was somehow possible to inherit my mother's inability to see who was—and who was not—good for me.

Sure, I stayed way the hell away from anyone who raised their voice at me, or in any way made me feel unsafe, but that didn't mean my choices were healthy, that I was able to make smart choices, that I had any skill at all in finding—yet alone being attracted to—the whole package.

On those thoughts, I fell into bed, passing out before I could make any sense of any of it.

I woke up feeling off-kilter, not sure if it was the same day or a week in the future, and certainly no clue if it was late at night or early in the morning.

Suddenly wide awake, I made my way to the bathroom, slipping into pajamas when I realized it was only a little after nine at night, then followed the lure of leftover mashed potatoes to the kitchen.

"Oh," I yelped, jumping back at the shirtless figure standing in the kitchen, half-obscured by the open refrigerator door, showing me just a sliver of back skin and his long gray sweatpants.

Oh, good God, not grey sweatpants.

Hadn't I been tormented enough?

"Hey, Princess," he greeted, closing the fridge door, shooting me a sheepish smile.

It took me a long second to find out why. Then my eyes landed on the giant plate on the island, loaded down with a slice of each of the pies from dessert.

My smile spread at that, a bit unexpectedly warm at the idea of him liking something I had made for him, finally understanding why my mother loved it so much.

THERE BETTER BE PIE

"Like that pie, huh?" I asked with a smile as I moved past him to drag the giant glass container of mashed potatoes out, dropping two—okay, three—heaping spoonfuls into a bowl, adding corn and gravy, then throwing it into the microwave.

"Surprised you're up. You couldn't have gotten much sleep last night. Then you were on your feet all day with that hangover."

"I think my body and mind teamed up to let me have just one last tradition," I told him, grabbing my food and a glass of apple cider, making my way out into the living room without saying anything else, while secretly hoping his curiosity was piqued enough to follow.

I didn't have to wait long.

"What tradition is that?" he asked, dropping down close to my spot.

Sure, it had the best view of the TV, but I was maybe wondering if he also wanted to be closer to me. Or if that was just wishful thinking.

"The best holiday movie ever made," I told him, flicking through my digital library. There wasn't much in it. Just all the best of all the Christmas movies. And this one special, underrated, personally beloved Thanksgiving one.

"*Home for the Holidays*," he repeated, clearly lost on what it was about.

"It's about this really dysfunctional family that is trying to hide the fact that it is so dysfunctional getting together for Thanksgiving. As you can guess, drama ensues. Hilarious, amazing, heart-warming drama. That is all you are getting out of me. And I now need quiet for approximately one-hundred-and-three minutes."

Then I went ahead and did the *thing*. You know the thing. When you convince someone to watch one of your favorite movies. And then spend half the runtime staring at them, watching them experience all your beloved characters and scenes.

I did that.

Like it was some kind of test.

THERE BETTER BE PIE

One that he passed with flying colors.

He laughed at the right spots, questioned the right things, looked suitably concerned in the sadder bits.

"Alright," I said as the credits rolled. "Let me have it."

"That was a good one," he told me, nodding, scraping his fork against the plate to get the last remnants of apple pie filling.

"I am afraid I am going to need more than that, Trip," I told him, watching as his lips curved up, eyes on me. Right when he put that fork in his mouth. And slowly pulled it back out, making sure he got every last bit off it.

My poor, poor system was not happy about the fact that I didn't just toss my bowl onto the table and jump him right then and there—taste the apple cinnamon still clinging to his lips and tongue.

"I am no film critic, but I think it is criminal I have never heard of this before. I mean, Robert Downey Jr. was amazing. And everyone played off one another perfectly. It had heart and humor and an epic Thanksgiving dinner blow up. I see why you watch it every year."

"Everyone always makes Christmas movies. They forget that all the great stuff that can happen at Christmas can also happen at Thanksgiving. I'm glad you liked it," I added, handing him my bowl when he reached for it, watching the way his body—with so little clothing covering it—moved as he folded forward to place our dirty dishes on the coffee table.

On the TV, the screen was back to the selection screen, silent.

The house was just as quiet.

But inside me, all I knew was chaos and noise.

The whooshing sound of my pulse in my ears, the thudding of my heart in my chest, the suddenly rapid intake and exhalation of breath, the swirling thoughts, too many of them to tell one from the other, to make sense of what they were trying to tell me.

All of them, though, were likely attempting to inform me that what I was about to do was idiotic, was a terrible, terrible idea.

But, well, I couldn't make out those thoughts.

So it really wasn't my fault.

I was just following the overpowering needs of my body.

That was why the second his back was against the cushions again, I was shifting up onto my knees, sliding over, moving to straddle his lap.

My gaze went to his, watching the confusion turn to heat, giving me the answer to all the questions I'd been wondering earlier about this situation being one-sided or not.

I wanted to linger, to commit the heavy-lidded look to memory.

But a part of me was acutely aware that the longer I paused, the more of a chance there would be for words to find their way to our lips.

And then who knows what might happen?

My hand planted on his shoulder—the skin hot, the muscles firm—and my lips sealed over his.

I'd felt tingles. Of course. I was a grown-ass woman. I'd known men in carnal ways before.

But this wasn't tingles.

This wasn't even fireworks.

This was something akin to bombs detonating through my system.

That was the only way I could think to describe it.

A whimper tore from somewhere buried deep, a sound drowned out by the rumbling, growling noise coming from Trip, something that vibrated through his body and into mine, sending a shiver through my system.

Trip's hands lifted from his sides, sinking into my ass, pulling me further up on his waist, high enough that I could feel his need pressing against my own.

Needy, shameless, my hips ground down against him, searching for some relief from the clawing need in my lower belly.

No longer needing to guide me, his hands slid up my spine, one hand sifting into the hair at the nape of my neck, curling, twisting, sending a delicious pain/pleasure tingling across my scalp.

His teeth nipped my lower lip, his tongue seeking entrance, then claiming mine, dragging a moan out of me as my hips did another grind.

It was the damn clock that did it.

The grandfather clock situated in the dining room.

The one that told us each time the hour changed.

The one that, to me, had become a sort of background noise over the years.

But Trip responded to it like it was cannon fire.

His hand released my hair.

His lips ripped from mine.

"Jett, no," he said, voice raspy with need, the need I still felt pressing against me, as my lips found the column of his neck. "Jett," he demanded again, voice gaining some firmness. "Stop," he added.

His hands sank into my hips, lifting, pushing me carelessly off to the side.

"We're not doing this," he told me, eyes forward, refusing to look me in the face as I tried to think through the haze of desire in my system.

"Trip..."

His name came out like a plead.

"Sorry, Princess. This is not happening. Don't try that again."

With that, he jumped up, rushed off, left me sitting there, his words like a slap across the face, leaving me reeling from the shock and the small surge of hurt.

I hadn't been the only one doing some kissing. His lips had been just as demanding as mine had. His hips had bucked up against mine, further stoking my need, promising release.

THERE BETTER BE PIE

I hadn't forced myself on him.

He'd been a willing—eager—participant.

Anger, a feeling I was much more comfortable with when it came to Trip, welled up, bubbled over, washing away the bulk of the need that had been overtaking me.

Don't try that again.

"Don't try that again?" I hissed, raking a hand through my hair.

Who the hell did he think he was?

And, what, he thought he was so irresistible that I would try to jump him after a rejection like that?

What an ass.

But of course he was an ass.

He had *always* been an ass.

Literally since the first day we met.

Thinking he was anything but was, well, the side effect of the holidays. I got wrapped up in the togetherness and the warmth and the traditions.

I had slapped on a pair of rose-colored glasses and moon-eyed someone I couldn't stand thee-hundred-and-sixty-something days of the year.

Well, the glasses were sure off now.

He wouldn't have to worry about me jumping him again.

Unless it was to strangle him.

That was a different—and much more likely—story.

I knew my parents wouldn't be happy about the one-eighty, were much more comfortable with the idea of Trip and I mending fences.

But, well, that was just something else I would have to deal with.

Because there was no way in hell I was going to be playing nice with Trip freaking Martin again.

Don't try that again.

Oh, he didn't need to trouble himself with that worry.

I'd never been more furious with the man before.

THERE BETTER BE PIE

Which was saying something since I had once contemplated murdering him with a chipped off piece of an ice sculpture. The evidence would have melted. No one would have been able to pin it on me.

On that note, I cleaned up our mess, and made my way back to my room, throwing myself down on my bed, running off a never-ending list of reasons to hate him, fueling the fire inside.

I didn't stop to think, however, of why it suddenly took so much work to try to find things about him that I didn't like when it used to be so easy.

And I damn sure didn't let myself contemplate the aching, ripped-open sensation located in the left side of my chest.

Nothing good could come from that.

CHAPTER EIGHT

Juliette

"You're up early," I observed, finding my father already up, dressed, and having his coffee on the back porch, watching the sun start to cast yellows and pinks across the seemingly never-ending sky.

I wasn't sure of the last time I had seen him awake before me. But, for a change, he had gone to sleep early the night before.

"That turkey knocked me out cold yesterday afternoon. I've been up for over an hour already. You off to take your walk?" he asked, nodding down at my travel mug in my gloved hand.

"Yeah. Gotta try to work off some of that food before we have another spread today."

"You two went even more overboard than usual," he agreed, but he wasn't complaining, that was for sure. The more food there is, the more times we could all enjoy it again. "Care for a little company?" he asked.

Involuntarily, something inside me seized at that, a strange sensation I needed to push down.

It wasn't that I didn't enjoy spending time with my father. In fact, I normally sought out rare moments when we could be totally alone together. It was no easy task given how popular a guy my father is.

But now, well, all that was on my mind was Trip recommending we drag the skeletons out from the closet, dust them off, and show them to each other.

He wasn't wrong. It was something that needed to happen. Our relationship hadn't been exactly the same since I had quit the company. We got along well for the most part. But the topic of work—his or mine—always tended to make us both get a little prickly.

While I did agree it was a talk we needed to have, I had maybe figured it would happen sometime down the road, that we were rarely alone, that I would never have that kind of conversation around my sensitive mother.

No one said we had to have the conversation now, though, even though we were going to be alone.

We could go at my pace.

When I felt ready.

"That'd be nice," I agreed.

"Trip told me you have a special spot with a fire pit."

"I do. It's my favorite spot out here," I agreed as we moved off into the woods.

"Would you show it to me?"

"Absolutely," I agreed.

Everything seemed fine at first.

We talked about the holiday, the plans for Christmas, what he was getting my mother even though she always insisted she had more than enough already, that he gave her the whole world.

You knew I was in a pissy mood when that thought—one that would normally make my heart feel all melty—made me grumble instead.

But then we got to my little spot.

My father got the fire started.

THERE BETTER BE PIE

I opened up my coffee to sip, taking a deep breath, enjoying the view.

And then he brought it up.

The very thing I didn't want to discuss.

"So, I am glad to see you and Trip putting aside your differences on this holiday. You're my little girl. He's my right-hand man. It makes your old man feel good to see you two getting along."

Then he was in for a bitter disappointment when we got back to the house, ran into Trip, and the iceberg that was between us tipped him off that we were back to our old ways.

A large part of me wanted to just tell him, lay it on the table, let him know that our momentary truce was just a dopamine-infused bout of insanity.

I knew, though, what would happen.

He would ask what had happened with us.

I didn't care how open you were with your parents, how comfortable you are with your own sexuality. No one, I repeat no one, wanted to tell their father that the reason you couldn't get along with his friend was because you jumped him on the couch, only to get rejected by him.

That would not go over well for anyone involved.

Not to mention it would be I-want-the-Earth-to-swallow-me-up humiliating.

So I went the chicken route. I decided to let him find out on his own. Preferably while my mother was around to act as a buffer to his anger over the whole situation.

"It's been an... enlightening trip," I told him, choosing the words carefully, refusing to lie to his face, but also not wanting to tell him too much of the truth.

"I'm happy to hear that," he agreed, nodding. "There is, of course, a reason other than my own sanity for wanting the two of you to be able to get along."

"Oh, really?" I asked, not sure what that reason could be. Other than wanting to save face in front of all his employees. Which was fair.

THERE BETTER BE PIE

"Yes. I actually—don't be mad at me—I discussed this with Trip a bit already actually. It's just—" He trailed off, raking a hand down his face that was getting redder from the cold by the moment. "I know work topics have been touchy for us for a long while now."

"I actually wanted to talk to you about that," I told him, happy for the segue, for the somewhat relaxed attitude he seemed to have about it at the moment.

"Good. I'm glad we are both ready to be open about this." He seemed to really mean that, too. My father wasn't exactly the mushy emotion kind of guy. While he was a talk-it-out sort much like I was, he didn't like when it got too wishy-washy, preferring it always stay a bit factual, leaving feelings out of it. "What did you want to talk to me about?"

My stomach contorted itself into a painful knot as I tried to find the right words to use to rip open this particular wound, one that had healed jagged and ugly, would fare better for the tearing and re-healing.

"I know you have never really understood why I up and left the company back when I did."

"No," he agreed, nodding. "I haven't ever understood that."

There was no thinking about the words that came next. They spilled out of me, raw, wet, ugly as they felt to keep them inside.

"I know you didn't want me. I know you wanted a son. I know you wanted to pass on the legacy to your son much like your father had done to you, like his father had done to him. I know that was always the plan. And I know I must have been a sore disappointment in comparison to that dream, to that planned legacy. I wanted it," I added, swiping the tear that refused to be contained off my cheek. "I had all these ideas and plans. But you never liked any of them. You never thought we thought the same way, saw the same future for the company. It was painfully clear to me that you didn't think I fit, but would never say that to me because of Mom and because you're a good person. But I *felt* it. I felt it

THERE BETTER BE PIE

and I just... it was ruining our relationship. If it went on, I knew that we would never be able to mend things. So the safest thing was... well... to just leave. To let you find someone else more suitable for your legacy."

There.

It was out.

At least I was pretty sure it was.

I might have blacked out a little bit somewhere in that long, rambling confession.

But I was confident most of the important parts were covered.

The silence after it, though, was deafening. And I couldn't seem to find the courage to make my gaze find his face, gauge his reaction. I just sat. Terrified. While he processed what I had dumped all over him.

After a moment or two, I was starting to worry that I would get no reaction out of him, that I had just blown up our entire relationship with one confession.

"Okay," he said finally, putting me out of my misery, allowing me to drag in one ragged breath that burned my cold lungs. "First of all, if there was ever anything I never said to you, not doing so had nothing to do with not wanting to hurt your mother, and everything to do with not wanting to hurt *you*, Juliette. And I have clearly not done my job as your father if you ever, for one minute, thought you weren't wanted, Jett. You were wanted."

"Mom was..."

"I loved your mother. I always loved your mother. You know that. But from the moment I knew you could possibly be mine, too, you were mine. I wanted you. And loved you. Not because you were part of your mother. But because you were part of the future I saw for all of us. Because of the family I knew we would become."

"You wanted..."

"A family," he cut me off. "We are a family. And you have never, not for one moment, been a consolation prize. You were wanted and loved every moment of your life. I won't lie and say that your mother and I didn't plan to

THERE BETTER BE PIE

have more children. You know we did. You know it was a blow to hear that doing so was not a possibility. But not because you weren't enough. You were—and are—enough for us. And I am sincerely sorry if you ever thought otherwise, if my words or actions or silence and inaction created that well of insecurity inside of you. You have to know that was never my intention. I love you, kiddo," he told me, reaching over to grab the arm that was bent to bury my sobbing face in my hands. "And you were— and are— very wanted."

I'm not sure I ever realized just how badly I needed to hear that, how much my soul was aching for that validation, those words of love and inclusion.

Having them, though, it pushed all those old feelings up and out, purging them like they needed, walling off the well they'd been living in, never to allow it to fill again.

"Now," he said after I managed to pull myself somewhat together with some deep breathing and horribly noisy sniffling. "As for the stuff about Kensley. I am not going to lie. You know that we never had the same vision for it. Not because we don't share blood, Jetty, but because we just see the world a little differently. It's not a bad thing. You know it has never been a bad thing. I implemented some of your suggestions to make the plant greener. We extended maternity leave, and created paternity leave. I have always given your ideas thought. And have put the ones that worked with my vision for the future to work for us. They have been some of our most widely praised changes. You made us a better company. But not in the same capacity you maybe had envisioned doing."

"'Sometimes expectations and reality don't line up,'" I said, parroting something I had heard him say many times over the years.

"Exactly. You were always a vital part of the team. In hindsight, though, I have to admit that I didn't always make that as clear to *you* as it always seemed to *me*. That is my mistake. I'm sorry for that too."

"It's okay," I told him, reaching to put my hand over his.

Incredibly, it was. Okay. I wasn't just feeding him platitudes, trying to make him feel better.

It was okay.

Pain purged, I was suddenly able to see things a lot more clearly than I had been able to when I'd been so consumed by it.

We'd both been at fault for keeping our mouths shut when the most constructive—and—cathartic thing would have been to speak our fears and frustrations, get them on the table to be discussed and moved on from.

Burying feelings never, ever, lead anywhere constructive.

"Feel a little better?" he asked, uncomfortably shifting his gaze over to the water.

"A lot better," I clarified, taking a deep breath. "Anyway, what did you want to talk to me about?"

"The future," he told me, nodding.

"The future of Kensley?" I clarified.

"Yes. And it involves both you and Trip."

I always knew it would involve Trip.

I didn't, however, see how I would play in.

"Me?" I asked, brows furrowing.

"I refuse to see a future of my company without you in it, Jetty."

"But... but we don't see the same way about it."

"No," he agreed, nodding, not one for lying to me. "But Trip does see the same future I do for it. So he would be in charge of the car features and models and such. You would be more in charge of the office stuff. The social media you are so good at. But to have the two of you at the helm, I would need you talking to each other. Without trying to rip each other's heads off. To set a good example for the employees. To keep things running smoothly."

He wanted me and Trip to co-run the company?

I was—at once—both incredibly moved.

And deeply horrified.

THERE BETTER BE PIE

We couldn't agree on the food at an event. And we were supposed to run a company together?

Add in the whole attraction and rejection thing.

It was the perfect recipe for a probable homicide if I ever saw one.

"You want Trip and I to run the company when you retire," I repeated.

"That is the dream I have for the future."

Honestly, it had been my dream as well. Minus Trip. Now that I knew it was a possibility again, I could see all the pieces of my life falling together.

I could move back to my hometown.

I could buy my fixer-upper.

I could work in the family business.

I could spend my free time with my mom redecorating my place.

I could have my parents over for Sunday dinners.

It was everything I had ever wanted.

Plus Trip.

It wouldn't be easy, but maybe I could learn to live with that. Work with him.

If it meant everything else I had ever wanted was to be mine.

"I like your dream, Dad," I told him, giving him a genuine smile, the kind that hurt my cheeks.

"I like it too," he agreed, clamping his hands on his knees. "Okay, what do you say we get back to the house? I'm sure your mother is up working on some dippy eggs right now."

"Dippy eggs are disgusting," I informed him, as I always did.

"I'm sure she will make you your eggies in a basket."

"I'm starving," I realized, falling into step beside him, letting myself lean into his side slightly. "I'm glad we cleared all this up," I told him as we were almost at the house.

THERE BETTER BE PIE

"Me too," he agreed, pressing a kiss to my temple in a show of affection he wasn't often known for.

"There you two are!" my mother cheered as we came in, smile bright. "I made dippy eggs," she declared, pushing a plate across the island toward my father who happily took it. "And one eggie in a basket," she told me as she took her plate to follow my father into the dining room. Almost seeming in a rush.

I couldn't figure out why at first until I saw Trip move into view.

"Were you crying?" he asked, brows low.

"No," I snapped, grabbing my plate, lying because the truth was none of his damn business.

"Bullshit, Princess," he shot back, gaze steady on mine as I forced my chin up, then plowed past him, choosing to take my food up to my room, needing a few minutes alone to try to work through my thoughts about the morning, about what it meant for my future.

Doing so around Trip was not going to be easy.

Sure, I would need to learn to get over that. We would have to coexist. Somewhat harmoniously.

To accomplish that, I figured our best bet was to avoid each other as much as possible. We couldn't argue if we didn't see each other.

To get everything I wanted, I could deal with him.

Maybe, some day, after some time had passed, we could actually get along. We'd proved it was possible. If we were both mature enough to keep personal feelings out of professional affairs, we could pull it off.

No one wanted us locked in an office, screaming our heads off about new model ideas or marketing plans, passions flaring, tempers flying.

Why my mind insisted on finishing that mental image with the idea of him bending me over the desk in my office was completely beyond me.

Because that was completely out of the question.
I didn't want that.
All that was over.

And even if maybe a teensy bit of the attraction was lingering, it damn sure had to be gone by the time we would need to start working together.

So what better way than to make sure it was over right this very moment?

The funny thing is, though, your mind can try to tell you one thing. But the other parts of you, yeah, they all have their own agenda.

CHAPTER NINE

Trip

I wasn't someone who experienced stress and anxiety.

Generally, I figured if there was a problem, I had to find a way to solve it. If there was a solution, there was no reason to stress about it. If there wasn't, then, well, you had to let it go.

It was easy for me.

But after the movie, after the kiss, after rejecting her, I took myself to my room, intent on just going to bed, thinking it all through in the morning.

Then went ahead and paced my room for hours.

Trying to figure out how things went so wrong so quickly.

I'd just wanted some pie.

I had planned to eat it in my room, then go back to bed.

Then there she was in those pink pajamas, getting this giant bowl of mashed potatoes, and going on about that movie and her tradition of watching it.

I wanted to tell myself that the only reason I wanted to watch it was because I was finding that I was enjoying new traditions, that I had been missing out on some awesome parts of the holiday season, that I wanted to see what more it had to offer.

The truth was, of course, that I really just wanted an excuse to be close to her, to see more of the things she enjoyed, to know what made her happy.

It was cheesy. Especially for me. No one would ever accuse me of being a romantic.

Yet that was how it was.

I wanted to see her favorite holiday movie.

I wanted to know if it was something I would like as well.

As it turned out, I did.

She had good taste in all things.

Really, I hadn't been fostering any ideas that something might happen between us because we were alone and in close proximity.

I wouldn't have let my mind go there.

Because it couldn't happen.

But then it did.

Fuck.

It was everything I imagined.

More, even.

I couldn't have known that Jett would be the sort of woman who instigated, who went ahead and took what she wanted. But, God, I had been given a treat.

I always figured that Jett would be the sort of woman who kissed like she fought. With everything in her.

I wasn't wrong.

Demanding, taking.

Grinding down against me.

Whimpering against my lips.

Every part of me wanted me to flip her over onto the couch, rip off both our bottoms, and bury deep inside her, get an end to the need that had been clawing at my system since the first time we'd argued with each other.

I might have, too.

If things stayed quiet, dream-like, a fantasy world of our own building.

Then the clock ruined it all.

Brought me back to reality.

Reminded me that this couldn't happen, that she was off-limits, that I couldn't let it go any further.

Regret and anger at the situation overtook my system, making me lash out, be harsh, needing to get away from her before I decided to screw the rules.

That didn't mean I enjoyed the look of shock on her face.

I damn sure didn't like the hurt and rejection that followed.

So then I paced.

There was no end to the anxiety, though, it seemed. My brain just kept racing around in endless circles, never settling on any solution, just replaying the whole thing until my brain and body were too exhausted to stay up for another minute.

When I woke up, I hadn't come to any new conclusions either.

The only solution I could come up with was to just act like nothing had happened. Just move on. She would be pissed at me, I figured. That seemed to be her go-to response to uncomfortable situations. At least regarding me.

Anger, I could live with.

Then she had walked into the kitchen with swollen eyelids, red eyes. Telltale signs of crying.

Crying.

I could handle pissed.

I couldn't handle upset.

I didn't even think I was capable of making her upset.

But there was no denying that was what she was.

I wasn't sure the last time I had felt quite as deflated as I did as I carried my breakfast into the dining room. Food prepared by the mother of a woman I had hurt. To sit down with the father of the girl I had hurt.

THERE BETTER BE PIE

Everything Kathy made tasted like gourmet. But the food might as well have been cardboard to me. I forced it down because of manners alone. I washed it down with hand-squeezed orange juice—something I'd never had before—and wasn't in the right headspace to appreciate right then.

"Heya, Trip," Mitch said as he followed me into the kitchen. "What do you say the two of us maybe do a little fishing?"

I didn't want to go fishing. I wanted to run up the stairs, barge into Jett's room, talk it out, apologize, tell her that I had never meant to hurt her, that it wasn't about her at all, that it was because of her father, because of my relationship with him, my respect for him.

I was starting to think I knew Jett enough to know, though, that she wouldn't be receptive to me being in her room. That she would not accept excuses or even an apology.

She would just yell.

Which would tip off her family that something was wrong. That, God forbid, something inappropriate had happened between us.

If I wanted to screw up a family Thanksgiving, I was pretty sure telling Mitch and Kathy that I had been dry humping their daughter on the couch in their family estate was the way to do it.

I couldn't talk to her.

At least not so soon.

I would drive myself crazy if I sat around all day thinking about it, too.

"Yeah, Mitch, that sounds like a good way to spend a few hours."

It was, too.

We talked business, about the future, about the upcoming holiday season.

We caught nothing.

But it did manage to drain most of the stress from my body.

THERE BETTER BE PIE

By the time we got back to the house, I was ready to face Jett again. Only to find Kathy alone in the kitchen preparing the leftovers for dinner.

"Where's my girl?" Mitch asked, pressing a kiss to the side of his wife's head.

"Oh, she's got a migraine. The poor thing. I told her I would make her a plate for her to warm up later if she feels better."

It was entirely possible, of course, that Jett did, in fact, have a migraine. I doubted it, though. It was more likely an excuse to avoid seeing me, dealing with me.

I wanted to be annoyed at her. For being a brat. For avoiding her family just because she couldn't be an adult and face me.

Those were words I would usually toss at her about the whole thing, too. Because it would give me the reaction I wanted from her.

Just this once, though, I decided to let it slide.

If I hurt her feelings, she deserved the space to be able to pull herself together about it. It wouldn't last forever. We still had several days around each other. She would have to face me sooner or later.

Or so I thought.

Dinner moved to dessert which moved to a couple drinks in front of the TV before Mitch and Kathy decided to call it a night around eleven.

Me, well, I couldn't sleep.

It was the chill that eventually dragged me out of bed. The supply of firewood in my room was down to nothing, making me make the trek from the deck and back inside to stoke my fire back to life.

The house was gorgeous, but it was drafty, poorly insulated. The fire barely managed to ward off the chill.

Once I got my fire going, my mind went back to Jett.

Up in the room that was likely even colder.
If I was out of firewood, she likely was too.

THERE BETTER BE PIE

Or, at least, that was the excuse I gave myself as I fetched more firewood, as I climbed two sets of stairs, as my knuckles gently knocked at the door.

Hearing nothing, I decided to let myself in, silently get her fire going, then slip back out.

With that, I pushed open the door, feeling the cold wall of air hit me, letting me know I was right to worry about her fire going out. Judging by the temperature—cold enough to make a shiver rack my usually overly warm system—it had been out for a long time already.

I tried to keep my focus on the task.

Given the initial darkness, this was not hard.

But by the time the fire was crackling happily, casting the room in a warm orange glow, there was no denying the fact that my gaze finally slid over to the bed, finding Jett buried beneath a giant pile of blankets, only her head and one full arm exposed, the arm cocked up over her forehead, pressing.

I knew that position from a mother who had suffered with seasonal migraines. The 'pressure makes it feel better' move.

She hadn't been lying about her headache.

And I felt like an ass for thinking she was so hung up on what happened with us that she was hiding away in her room.

Realizing I was invading her privacy, I went to make my way toward the door, foot catching the floorboard I often heard her step on when she was moving around, one that made a wince-worthy groaning sound when you put pressure on it.

Jett was not an overly deep sleeper.

She jolted almost violently awake, voice gasping inward as she shot up in bed.

"It's me, Princess," I told her, voice soft, reassuring.

"Trip? What the hell... why are you here?" she asked, making me take a step to the side, allowing her to see the fire dancing around happily, already filling the room with warmth that hadn't been there a moment before.

"Sorry, didn't mean to wake you. I ran out of firewood. I wanted to check if you did too. You did."

"You... you built me a fire?" she asked, brows pinching over swollen, unfocused eyes.

"I know it gets cold in this house," I told her, feet shifting, a little uncomfortable with her penetrative glance.

"I... thank you," she said, looking over at the fire, wincing.

"Did you take anything? Want me to grab you something?"

"Nothing works," she said, shaking her head, telling me the same thing my mother used to. "They just make me even more nauseated. I can usually sleep through them. What time is it?"

"A little after ten," I told her, watching as she calculated how long she'd been asleep.

"I slept all day."

"Pretty much."

"I'm still tired."

"Go back to sleep," I suggested, shrugging.

"I can't."

"Why not?"

"Because you're standing there staring at me," she said, eyes rolling a bit before she fell back on the pillows with a grumble, throwing her arm over her forehead once again.

"Good night, Princess," I murmured, making my way to the door.

"Thank you, Trip. For the fire," she clarified.

I closed her door feeling a wave of relief wash through me.

If we could be civil when she suddenly found me invading her personal space without permission, I had a lot of hope for the next several days.

We would be able to get along well enough to fool her parents.

And then we could all just go back to our lives.

Or so I told myself.

So I thought.
As it turned out, fate had other plans in mind.
Well, fate.
As well as Kathy and Mitch.

CHAPTER TEN

Juliette

Crippling, soul-sucking migraine gone, I woke up feeling like a new person, which was usually the case after a headache put me down in bed unable to open my eyes because when I did, my stomach rolled and threatened to empty its meager contents, for half—or a whole—day.

My eyes still felt a little swollen, I was dehydrated, and I was starving, but I felt great as I rushed through my shower, got dressed, then made my way down the stairs, ready to head straight to the fridge to have leftovers at six in the morning.

Not even the sight of Trip already in the kitchen, holding a cup of coffee, leaning a bit over the island—and likely ready to pick at me about something—was enough to dull my mood.

"Hey, Princess. We got a problem," he said, pushing a sheet of paper across the island toward me as I approached.

One glance told me my mother had left a note. I had seen her handwritten notes on the island hundreds of times over the years in that swirling, perfect penmanship that made my own chicken scratch look like a child had done it.

"Problem?" I repeated, grabbing the note.

Pudge & Trip - Sorry to have to leave so abruptly, but we had a pressing issue sprung on us all of a sudden. We would have waited for you two to wake up, but the weather station claimed we were in for an unexpectedly intense snow shower. We needed to get on the road early to get ahead of it. Please stay for the rest of the holiday. Finish up the food. Enjoy the ambiance. We will call when we are back home.
Love always, Mom and Dad.

Something about the phrase 'unexpectedly intense snow shower' had my stomach twisting.

Now, I loved snow.

I loved snow as much as a kid who woke up to watch the news to find their district had closed for the day.

But an 'unexpectedly intense snow shower' sounded like it might be the kind of thing that would make it absolutely impossible to avoid Trip should we start butting heads once again. Which, given our history, seemed more like an eventuality than a possibility.

"'Unexpectedly intense snow shower,'" I repeated aloud, glancing up to find Trip turning to walk toward the living room.

"Already on it," he told me, grabbing the remote, flicking on the TV to the weather station.

Without even grabbing a coffee first, I moved into the living room, waiting for them to finish a rambling about the snow preparedness, before getting back to the actual snow forecast.

"That can't be right," I blurted out, seeing the numbers.

"This is Maine. We're like a skip and a jump from Canada here..."

"Yeah, but there is never snow like that at this time of the year! The most we have ever gotten is like two or

THERE BETTER BE PIE

three inches over the Thanksgiving holiday. Ten to twelve inches is insane."

Ten to twelve inches sounded like—even if we managed to shovel out the giant, sprawling driveway—we might have to wait three or four days at least before the main road was cleared since it was practically a private drive given that only my parent's home was off of it, and it was clearly not going to take top priority.

"Well, at least we know we won't starve," he said, shrugging it off, not the least bit concerned about the possibility of us strangling each other at some point in the very near future because we were trapped together with no one else to buffer our tumultuous moods and outbursts.

Food was the least of my worries as I made my way back to the kitchen, pouring a coffee, putting my usual sugar and syrup in it before going to the fridge to get the milk

It was right about then that I realized something was amiss.

That maybe my sainted mother was not quite so innocent after all.

Because we had been on the last half of the milk.

But now there was an extra gallon tucked away in the back.

The rational part of my brain told me that I was probably being paranoid, that I likely had just missed the extra gallon of milk, that there had been so many leftovers tucked away that I may have missed it.

That rational part of me wanted me to believe that because I had never known my mother to be a liar. In fact, she was honest to a fault. I learned the truth about Santa because, at seven, I had asked a really innocent question about why she had wrapping paper in her closet that matched my Christmas presents. Whereas other parents may have fumbled before croaking out something about how Santa asked them to provide wrapping paper this year, my mother blushed and cried and told me the truth right then and there.

THERE BETTER BE PIE

The other part of my brain, though, felt like something was off, and went in search of confirmation.

It didn't take long.

There were more oranges. When my mother had complained just the morning before that she was out.

There was a new—sealed—tub of whipped butter.

And fresh bagels on the counter.

My father always watched the weather before bed.

He had to have known this was coming.

He would have shared that with my mother.

Who then hatched a plan to—what—escape while they could while leaving us to fight it out?

That did not sound like her.

But what other excuse could there be?

They had to have left before the sun was even up, gone down to town, come back with supplies, then packed up and left.

To what end, though?

"What's that look for?" Trip asked, head cocked to the side as my mind raced from here to there and back again.

"I, ah—" I mumbled, not wanting to implicate my mother in case I did happen to just have it all wrong. "I need to get out of here," I decided, wondering how quickly I could get my bags re-packed, get down the hill, and even just, I don't know, get a hotel room until the storm passed so that I could go home.

"Too late, Princess," Trip told me, making me turn back to my race up to my room.

"Too late?" I repeated, finding him waving an arm out toward the windows.

And, sure enough, there were the fat tufts of snow already steadily starting to fall from the sky.

"Noooo," I whimpered, shoulders falling.

It was coming down hard already. Even if I did grab my stuff and head out, the roads would already have a coating. Driving on them even in good weather was nerve-racking with their narrowness and tendency toward twisting at obnoxious angles.

I maybe didn't want to be stuck with Trip—alone—but I didn't want to escape it only to end up in a coffin either.

"I thought you liked snow?"

"I *love* snow," I corrected. "I am not too keen on being trapped because of it," I admitted.

"Trapped with me, you mean," he clarified, but didn't seem offended either.

"Well, yeah," I told him, shaking my head. "I mean, you can't be thrilled about this either."

"Thrilled, no. Especially if you are going to be a pain in the ass about it."

"I am not being a pain in the ass! We can hardly even discuss the *weather* without arguing, Trip. The weather. The most innocuous topic known to mankind."

"We aren't arguing about the weather. We are debating the implications of being stuck with each other. Which is a different topic."

"We are probably going to be trapped for *days*, Trip."

"Yeah," he agreed, nodding. "That seems likely."

"And you're okay with that?"

"I recognize that there isn't anything we can do about it. So there is no reason to stress out about it. And grind your teeth about it," he added a bit pointedly.

There was always a reason to stress out about things. Or, at least, that was how my mind liked to operate. I could always find something to freak out about, to keep me up at night, to keep my mind occupied until I worked myself up to an anxiety attack.

I envied people who didn't have minds that worked that way. People like my parents who could go right to sleep even after a major dip in the stock market that could potentially really impact their savings and Kensley Automobiles. I would have managed to worry myself to an ulcer over the whole thing only to wake up the next

THERE BETTER BE PIE

morning—after a scant forty minutes of sleep—to find the market right back up, and realize I had made myself sick over nothing.

But that was just how I worked.

I worried.

I considered all the ways any potential situation could be worse. Then imagined each and every one of those things coming true.

"Princess, what is the worst that could happen?" he asked, shrugging.

"I could stab you to death with a very dull kitchen knife," I told him, watching as he smiled at that.

"That is a possibility," he agreed, nodding. "I won't lose sleep over it, though. What else?"

"We could run out of food."

"And, what, Donner party each other? I think we're safe in that front too, Jett. What else?"

What else?

Well, I could lose my freaking mind and jump him again. Get rejected by him again. Die of complete and utter mortification over the whole ordeal.

That could happen.

But I couldn't exactly say that to him, now, could I?

"Exactly," he said, nodding. "We will hang out here, watch the snow, eat food, shovel out the driveway, and hopefully not resort to using dull butter knives to eviscerate each other."

"I mean... the last one is going to be difficult," I told him, lips twitching.

"You'll just have to try your best, Princess," he told me, eyes dancing.

Alright.

Maybe it wouldn't be so bad.

He was right.

If you had to be trapped by an epic snowstorm, there were much worse situations to find yourself in. Stuck in your car at the side of the road. At work, surrounded by coworkers you just barely managed to tolerate for eight hours a day. Or with your therapist who increasingly lost their professionalism until they were on the floor sobbing about how their father had two families at the same time while they were growing up, and you realized that if you ever get out of said situation, you would need to start all over again with a new therapist because you would never be able to get the image of them hugging a pillow to their chests and calling for their absent fathers to come save them out of your head.

Shit could always, always be worse.

We had a beautiful house, food, water, firewood, and working cable. At least for the time being.

All said and done, it wasn't a bad situation.

I just needed to try to take a page out of my mother's book, and try to be more optimistic.

Besides, if things did go south, it wasn't like we were trapped in a closet together; we could each go off to our own rooms and avoid each other like the plague.

It would be fine.

"How's your head?" Trip asked as the silence trudged on.

"Better. Thank, God. That was a good one. And by good, I clearly mean bad."

"Maybe triggered by the crying," he said, choosing his words carefully, trying to—I don't know—probe a bit without seeming like that was what he was doing.

He wasn't wrong.

My migraines had a lot of triggers. Some more obvious than others. Drastic changes in temperatures, coming rain, too little sleep, too much eye strain from being on the computer without enough breaks.

And, well, crying.

Not just tearing up over a greeting card commercial about a sad old man or a lonely dog.

No.

But the kind of bawling that left you red-streaked and swollen.

Like I'd had the day before.

THERE BETTER BE PIE

It may have been cathartic, something that lifted a weight, eased a burden, cauterized a wound that wouldn't stop bleeding, destroying everything I knew and loved.

But that didn't mean I felt great after.

In fact, I felt wrung out and tired.

Then the tension in my jaw started, followed by the tight feeling across my forehead, the little specks in my vision—auras—that were always a precursor to a really bad migraine. The kind that crippled your whole life until it finally decide to release its grasp on you.

"Yeah," I agreed, turning to pretend that getting out some leftovers required the utmost attention. "That can be a factor."

"Look," he said, voice suddenly serious, deep, firm. "I get that I maybe bruised your pride a little, but there really is no need to cry over that situation."

"Oh. My. God," I said, each word its own sentence, momentarily making me resemble the most misunderstood—and unfairly criticized, in my humble opinion—character from *Friends*. "Are you serious right now?" I asked, face scrunching up. "I mean... how arrogant do you have to be to think I was off in the woods crying over a nothing kiss with you?

"I'm not judging you for it," he went on, shaking his head.

"Wow. You need to get over yourself," I told him, putting the lid back on the food I had been opening, suddenly finding I had lost my appetite. At this rate, I would be the only person walking away from Thanksgiving weighing less than they had going in. "Not everything is about you."

"No? What were you crying about then?"

"I don't owe you explanations."

"Then I will have to go on assuming it was about me."

"It was about my father!" I snapped. I didn't want to give him the satisfaction of the truth, but the idea of him thinking I was heartsick over him was even more unpalatable. "Not that it is any of your business."

"Mitch made you cry?" he asked, eyes scrunching small.

"Not intentionally," I clarified. "But yes. We had a talk. A long overdue one."

"Well, good. And also, you're welcome."

"For what?"

"For encouraging you to talk to him about it."

"You mean snap at me and make me feel really silly and childish for daring to have feelings about my upbringing?"

"I didn't *make* you feel anything. You chose that. You can't blame someone else for your reactions to what they may say."

"We're not talking about someone else. We're talking about you. And I do think I have the right to feel like crap about something you said when your sole intention was to make me feel like crap."

"If you really think that was my intention, Princess, you don't know anything about me."

"I know you seem to have this sick need to provoke me whenever you find a chance."

To that, he was silent for a long moment. Almost as if he was, I don't know, searching for a lie or evasion he could feed to me. Since we both knew it was the truth. For some unknown reason, he liked poking at me, getting a reaction, starting a fight then seeing it through until we were almost ready to strangle each other.

"Maybe you're just too easily provoked," he suggested, shrugging.

"You're literally the only person who provokes me like this."

"So stop giving me so much real estate in your head."

He made it sound so easy.

It was not that easy.

That wasn't how the brain worked.

THERE BETTER BE PIE

At least, it wasn't how *my* brain worked.

I took a breath so deep it burned, letting out slowly.

"Okay. How about we start over?" I suggested.

"Start over?" he asked.

"Hi, I'm Juliette Kensley. Yes, *that* Kensley. But I work at a makeup company and use coupons when I shop. Also, everyone calls me Jett," I said, reaching out my hand toward him.

His brow raised, but he decided to play along. "Trip Martin. I hear that *some* people call me Trip *Freaking* Martin*,*" he added, and I felt heat rise up my neck and bloom across my cheeks. "I work with cars. Most people think I am a pretty pleasant guy. Oh, also, I like apple pie."

"How interesting. I *make* the best apple pie known to mankind."

"You really do," he agreed, giving me that easy smile so many others got graced with, but I had only been given a handful of times over the years.

"Is there any left?" I asked, watching as he went sheepish as a little boy caught with his hand in the proverbial cookie jar. "You ate the rest of it?"

"I wouldn't be opposed to you baking another."

"You're not going to fit into your pants by the time we get the hell out of here."

"I have that giant driveway to shovel a foot of snow off of. I need sustenance."

"I'll help with the driveway."

"You will?"

"Try not to look so shocked, Trip. I also do my own laundry. And even change my own oil in my car."

"Bullshit," he said, shaking his head.

"Not bullshit. My father refused to let me drive a car until I knew the basics of how one works and how to take care of it. That car out there might be a POS, but that oil is fresh, the air filters are clean, and the tires are rotated."

Something crossed his face, a look that I was finding hard to place. Interest, maybe. But there was something more lively there. Something, I don't know, maybe even a little heated?

No.

Clearly, that didn't make any sense.

"You change your own oil? You. Who is worth millions."

"Really, we're back to that again?"

"I'm not judging you, Jett. I'm trying to understand. Why get your hands dirty when you could pay someone to change it?"

"Because it is the one way my father and I have been able to still bond after I left the company. I drive back to Pennsylvania to visit. We take my car out to his garage, get it up on some ramps, look it over together."

"That's a nice tradition," he told me, nodding. "But I think the two of you are going to have a lot of ways to connect with each other in the coming years."

It sounded like he knew.

"Did my father talk to you about his dream for Kensley?" I asked.

"Yeah, he did. Only for a minute. He knew your mom would be pissed if we talked business over a holiday, so we didn't get too far into it."

To that, my lips curved up. "If you think my mother is even remotely capable of being 'pissed,' then you don't really know her very well."

"That's true. You'd think she'd have more. With the life she had led before Mitch."

"My mom has been through a *lot* of therapy. Before I was born, especially, wanting to make sure her trauma didn't negatively affect me. But she continued it on even after. And then when they opened the clinic, she started going to the weekly group sessions on top of that. She has really worked on herself and healed the wounds of the past. And, I think, having something like she and my father have is its own kind of healing too."

"I've never seen anyone like them. Not with so many years in."

"Me either," I agreed. "He looks at her like she is the sole reason the sun rises in the morning."

"That is exactly how he looks at her," he agreed. "And she is always leaning into him, reaching for his hand, finding some reason to touch him."

"It's something to aspire to, that's for sure," I agreed, feeling the ache of longing.

"You want that?" he asked, eyes guarded.

"I have a full life," I told him, knowing it was true. "I have a rewarding career, friends, an amazing family. I, yeah, I would like a partner. It would be nice to have someone to share all of that with, build on that with."

"In your fixer-upper?"

"Yeah. In my fixer-upper."

"Why fixer-uppers?" he asked, genuinely curious.

"I don't know," I admitted. "I think a case could be said for my mother's background. She went to school for decorating. But I think there is something about, I don't know, seeing the potential that everyone else misses, I guess. It is easy to love something that is already perfect. But sometimes, you can see what is perfect underneath all the crap when no one else can. And that is more rewarding, I think. Things you have to work for always end up being the most rewarding."

"I think I am starting to get you, Princess," he said, eyes thoughtful, voice softer than I was used to.

"What do you mean?"

"I dunno. You were kind of born into the perfect house, y'know? It was perfect. It required nothing of you. You could have easily stayed there, gotten comfortable, let everyone come in and look around in awe. But that wasn't good enough. You wanted to earn it, to get the reward of all that hard work. I get that. I respect that."

"Do you feel that?" I asked, reaching my arms out a bit dramatically.

"Feel what?" he asked, tensing.

"I think hell is freezing over," I told him, watching as his shoulders fell again as he snorted. "Trip Freaking

Martin *respects* me. Oh, how far we have come from that time you once told me to go cry in my private plane."

His head ducked at that. "I didn't say that."

"No," I agreed. "Actually, I think you said my yacht."

"In my defense, Princess, I didn't know you then."

"You didn't want to."

"I did, actually," he corrected.

"Wait... really? Why?"

"Because everyone loved you. And I figured if you were Mitch's kid, you must have been pretty amazing. But then you decided to hate me."

"You insulted my idea!"

"I was trying to agree with Mitch. I have nothing against electric cars. Some luxury companies are doing well with them. But I think we both have to agree that most people—not even those who could afford them—are going to want electric cars. There are too many dead zones where you can't charge. Repairs cost several limbs. They're great. But not overly practical just yet."

"So you could see Kensley having an electric car in the future? Not to replace an old model, but to add to the fleet."

"In another five years, yeah, I think I could see that."

"Are you just agreeing with me because, in the future, we will have to work together, and you think kissing my ass might work in your favor?"

"Jett, babe, if there is one thing you can always count on with me, it is that I am going to give you the truth. No matter how much you might hate to hear it. I am not going to lie to you or kiss your ass in order to try to save my own. That's not who I am. And, I don't think that is someone you want working beside you either."

"No," I agreed, nodding, pretending to ignore the little flutter in my belly at the word *babe*. "I like the truth. Even if it hurts."

THERE BETTER BE PIE

"The truth right now is, if this shit keeps up," he said, waving an arm behind him toward the windows, "our arms might fall off from exhaustion while shoveling that driveway."

"My father always claims it is best to go out in shifts, getting ahead of it before it all falls. I don't know if there is actually any validity to that plan, though."

"Then let's err on the side of laziness," he suggested with a mischievous smirk. "We still have leftovers to finish before they go bad."

"That's true. And it would be really terrible to waste food."

"And a perfectly comfortable couch is useless if no one is sitting on it," he agreed.

"You know what, I like the way you think," I told him, finding I actually meant it. "If you want, I can introduce you to my personal favorite invention," I told him.

"Well, now, I have to know what that is, don't I?"

"I call it a Thanksgiving pierogi," I told him.

"I'm not hating the sound of that."

"You make the dough for pierogi, then you layer it with mashed potatoes, stuffing, corn, turkey, and gravy, then pinch it all closed, bake it, and eat."

"That sounds so awful that it has to be amazing."

"It *is*. My mom hates it. But my dad and I usually eat them when the leftovers are winding down. It uses up all the ingredients, but tastes different."

"How long until I can have one?" he asked, placing a hand on his stomach.

"That depends. Are you a 'breakfast is for breakfast and dinner is for dinner' type of person, or do you throw all the food rules out the window?"

"Breakfast-for-dinner was always my favorite as a kid."

"Oh, good. A fellow food rebel. Well, then... I can make them now."

"What can I do?"

"Not get in my way," I suggested, making him smile. "And maybe pick out a good Christmas movie."

"*Die Hard* it is."

"That is not a Christmas movie."

"Is so. The best one."

"Bruce Willis says it isn't a Christmas movie."

"What does he know?"

"He's the star of it!"

"If being the star of something makes that person an expert in that field, Princess," Trip shot back, "then Russel Crowe must be great at gladiating."

"'Gladiating' isn't a word," I told him, rolling my eyes.

"The movie takes place on Christmas."

"*Goodfellas* has a Christmas scene. But I think we can all agree it is not a Christmas movie."

"You're a pain in the ass, babe," he said, but he was grinning while he did it.

"You should be used to that by now," I shot back.

"I think I am," he agreed. "Alright, fine. How about... *Trapped In Paradise*."

"Oh, an obscure one. I like it. Sounds like a plan."

"I'll go find it."

"Hey, Trip," I called as he started away, making him turn back.

"Yeah?"

"We just disagreed without jumping down each other's throats."

"It's a nearly-Christmas miracle," he agreed, shooting me a smile that made my knees forget how they worked for a second. Luckily, he was already turning away and making his way toward the living room, and didn't see me have to hold onto the counter to keep myself upright.

Alone, my gaze slid over to the nearly-forgotten note on the island.

That mother of mine was a devious woman.

It hadn't simply been wishful thinking on her part.

About Trip and me.

She'd seen something there.

She knew that if we could just stop screaming at each other, we might actually find we really enjoyed each other's company.

And she knew that the only way for us to come to that realization on our own was to book it out of town, and leaving us abandoned and trapped by an epic snowstorm.

My mother, the hopeless romantic.

My gaze slid over toward the living room, looking at Trip, feeling a warm sensation spreading across my chest.

Apparently, like mother, like daughter.

CHAPTER ELEVEN

Juliette

"What the hell are you doing?" Trip asked from behind me, making me jolt, sliding a foot across the slippery back deck. My entire life flashed before my eyes, focusing a little too long on that one time in middle school when I didn't realize my shirt had been tucked into my *underwear* at school, as my belly dropped, making me shriek, arms flying out to try to steady myself, making me drop my towel.

Luckily, I saved the wine.

"I am making the best of this never-ending snow," I declared.

"By losing your damned mind?" he asked, brows furrowed, incredulous gaze moving over the giant floor-length, three sizes too big robe that belonged to my father, the wine, the bright, multicolored umbrella in my hand.

"By having some fun," I corrected.

"Are you drunk?"

"Not yet," I declared, opening the umbrella, jamming it into a snow-filled planter.

"Alright. Then what are you doing?"

THERE BETTER BE PIE

"I have always had this weird dream to go in a hot tub in the snow," I told him. "And since this is the Snowmageddon, and we might not ever be making it out of here, I figured I might as well strike this off my bucket list. Are you just going to stand there, or are you going to help me with this cover?" I asked, unclasping the buckles.

"You're going to give yourself hypothermia." But he came over and hauled off the top for me.

"In a hot tub? Unlikely," I told him, taking the steadying breath I knew I would need for courage as I set down the wine bottle, then reached for the knot of my train.

I ripped the robe open with a quick burst of bravery, feeling the cold immediately nip at every inch of skin, the snow falling on my shoulders, making a shiver rack through my system.

But one glance at Trip managed to make an entirely different kind of shiver move through me.

Because there was no mistaking the hunger in his eyes as his gaze moved over my nearly-nude body, focusing for a long moment on my nipples that were poking through the thin fabric.

Quickly, though, the cold turned to little knives attacking every inch of exposed skin, making me need to seek refuge from it, dropping myself down into the hot water with a sigh.

"I'm trying to figure out the umbrella," Trip declared, pointedly looking away, voice a little rougher than usual.

"Well, the dream was to, you know, be in a hot tub with snow falling all around. But, well, the more rational part of me said that maybe freezing cold and wet hair and a hot body was a recipe for a ruined experience. This way, my head stays dry, I stay warm, and everything is a win-win," I told him, reaching for the bottle of wine with arms made weak from what seemed like endless shoveling from the past day and a half, taking a quick swig.

"It's a fair plan," he agreed, nodding, standing there with his hands tucked into his pockets.

THERE BETTER BE PIE

"Are you going to come in or what?" I asked, looking up at him.

I couldn't claim to be a good flirter, someone who was coquettish by nature. But I was pretty sure I managed to pull off a subtle eyelid flutter paired with some heavy lids, daring him to come in, to get close to me.

And, amazingly, it worked.

He shucked off his sweatshirt, slipped out of his shoes and pants, leaving him just in his boxer briefs that left *very* little to the imagination, and jumped in just as the goosebumps rose up on every inch of skin, leaving me wishing he'd paused for just a moment longer as the water distorted him completely.

"I should have told you to grab some beer," I said, reaching for the bottle of wine to take another swig.

"I'll have to make do," he said, reaching to take the bottle from my hand, lifting it to his lips.

That was just the tipping point for me.

For a day and a half, I had been with him side-by-side without a single argument—even though we'd disagreed on several topics. We'd eaten my Thanksgiving pierogi, which were a big hit. We watched movies, cleaned, shoveled, did the dishes, played cards—where I found out to my utter delight that he was an atrocious bluffer—for lack of anything else to do, shoveled some more. He kept me company while I baked him another apple pie, this time feeling that same sensation I thought my mother must have felt when she made my father his pecan pies every year. We'd shoveled once again. Then we talked a bit about Kensley going forward without—and this was a miracle—raising our voices, always hearing each other out. Then we'd gone to sleep.

Well, I assumed *he* had gone to sleep.

I had been up tossing and turning with an aching need in my core.

Somewhere in there, I had come to the conclusion that I was really starting to like Trip. If I were being completely honest with myself, I had maybe even always liked him a little bit all along. Yes, even when I'd been fighting with him. I liked that he could keep up with me in an argument, that he somehow always managed to take the edge off some of his jabs by making them funny, how he refused to back down regarding what he was passionate about.

And, yeah, let's not forget that he had always been the best looking guy I had ever seen.

That maybe my mother was right all along about needing passion to fight the way we did.

Passion was absolutely what I was feeling as I watched him place the bottle down, momentarily distracted with that task, clearly missing the intent behind my eyes.

I was not, generally, the make-the-first-move kind of person. I was happy to instigate once I was with someone for a while, but I had never had the confidence to handle potential rejection. I had certainly never made a second move after my first one *was* rejected. Somewhat brutally, I might add.

I guess a part of me just had to know.

If I got rejected again, I was sure—or, at least, partially sure—I could put it all to rest. Move on. Forget it happened. Continue to be cordial with him, so that when the time came to take over the company, it was a smooth transition.

With that confidence, I took a breath, pushed off my side of the hot tub, floated over toward his, watching as realization crossed his face.

The heat that flooded his eyes was really the only encouragement I needed.

My bare legs slipped over his bare legs, the sensation intimate, making my thigh muscles tense as my knees rested on the sides of his hips on the small seat he was situated on. My hips glided forward, sinking down. With very little between us, I could feel his need starting to match my own.

"Don't," I demanded softly when his lips parted, sure he was about to object.

"You're Mitch's daughter," he told me.

"Oh." The sound rushed out of me, releasing the insecurity I had been harboring from what I thought had been a rejection.

"Oh?" he repeated.

"Yeah," I agreed, feeling a smile pull at my lips. "Oh. I get it now."

"You get what now?"

"It's just... here I was, all insecure that you had rejected me because you just... didn't want me."

"Didn't want you," he repeated, blowing his air out of his nose. Then his hips rose up, grinding his hardness against me. "Does it feel like I don't want you, Princess?"

No.

No, it didn't.

"You just don't want to because of my father?" I specified.

"Yeah, babe. I respect your father too much to fuck around with his daughter."

"Trip, my parents didn't have a pressing matter back home," I told him, feeling my lips curve up at the confusion wrinkling his brow. "You didn't notice that they had headed down into town to stock us up first?" I asked, watching as that confusion turned to suspicion.

"No."

"Yeah, they did. And they rushed out of here at the crack of dawn after. My dad watches the news and weather before bed. He would have known this was coming. They probably went to bed planning it. My dad would run to town. My mom would pack up and load the car. Then they would get out of here before we got up and before the snow started. This was their doing. This was what they wanted."

"You think your parents are secretly trying to hook us up, Jett? They know we hated each other."

"My mom was hinting about how there was a thin line between love and hate. And how it took a lot of passion to fight like we were always fighting. She rushed out of the room anytime we were in there, trying to give us more time alone."

"Alright. Maybe I can see your mom being in on it. She wants you to find someone. To settle down. To have what she has. But not Mitch."

"No?" I asked, brow lifting. "He wants us to run his company. He wants us to be his legacy. And what would be more perfect for that than if we decided we didn't hate each other after all, and wanted to get together?"

"Hm."

"Right?" I agreed, nodding. "So... maybe I'm not so off-limits after all," I told him, ducking my head down, pressing my lips into his cool neck, feeling the shiver that coursed through him at the contact.

"I mean... if this is their wish," he said, voice already getting rough, and that need of his was pressing hard and demanding at the juncture of my thighs.

"Interpersonal relations are very important," I agreed, lips closing around his earlobe, making his hips jerk upward, his cock pressing into my throbbing clit.

"Anything for the company," he agreed, lips crushing down on mine, making anymore talking—or even thinking–possible.

My hips ground down on his as his teeth nipped my lower lip, dragging a ragged moan from buried somewhere deep.

My arms wrapped around his neck, his sank into my ass, helping me rock against him, driving me up, sure release was just one more stroke away.

"Wait, wait," he demanded, pulling me back, chuckling at the grumble I let out when his fingers sank into my hips, pushing my body back, away from him. "We need to get inside," he told me.

Rationally, I knew he was right.

But the last thing my desperate body wanted in that moment was to be rational. It just wanted a blissful end to the clawing sensation in my lower belly.

"This was the part of the plan I really didn't think through," I admitted, grimacing as my gaze moved around to the snow already coating my robe, his clothes, the shoes I had kicked out of.

"We're just going to have to make a run for it," Trip said, reading my dread.

It was the only way.

"On three," I said, pulling away from him, reaching down to grab his hand. "One... two... two-and-a-half..."

I didn't get to three.

Trip's hand crushed mine as he flew up out of the hot tub, practically dragging me with him. I didn't even manage to grab my robe or towel, didn't get to slip my feet into my shoes.

A thousand blades sliced at my skin at once as we darted across the twenty or so feet from the hot tub to the back door, throwing ourselves inside.

"That was so much worse than I imagined," I whimpered, grabbed the blanket off the back of the couch, wrapping it around myself.

"You're just going to let me freeze?" he asked, looking around for another blanket, finding none.

"Come on in," I invited, opening up the side, sliding my arm around his lower back as he pulled it just barely around our two bodies. "This is awkward," I declared as we both fell into step with all the grace of a couple of five-year-olds in a three-legged race.

As we made our way up the steps, I realized just how very unsexy this whole plan was. I had not really thought it through.

And now, it seemed, the mood was gone.

A soaking wet race through freezing temperatures with steadily falling snow was a great libido killer.

"This is your stop," I reminded him when we got toward his door. "I would like to be the bigger person, but I am keeping the blanket," I informed him, feeling the shivers rack my system.

THERE BETTER BE PIE

"Bringing you up," he informed me, leading me up. "I won't let you fall down," he told me, pulling me a little closer.

"I hate these stairs."

"I noticed," he agreed, pushing open my bedroom door.

The fire was still crackling, and Trip led me over toward it, pushing me down, stepping out of the comfort of the blanket, walking off toward my bathroom.

From my position, I caught a glimpse of his back as he went into the linen closet to grab towels, rubbing one over his shoulders, chest, and back.

And then, oh, then, he reached down, grabbing his soaked boxer briefs, yanking them down off his legs, letting them fall toward the floor, leaving me with a perfect view of his glorious ass for a long moment before he wrapped the towel around himself, tucking it at his hip, before turning, making his way back toward me.

There was something intense in his eyes, something that had me keeping my mouth shut, going with it as he lowered down in front of me, reaching up to gather my hair to one side of my neck, using the towel to dry off the ends that had drifted into the water.

Finished with that, his hands eased the blanket off my shoulders, using the towel to dry my shoulders and upper back, reaching behind me to undo the clasp of my bathing suit top, carefully dragging it down.

That libido that had taken a hit from the Arctic run roared back to life, burned even hotter.

My normal instinct would be to brush him off, assure him that I could dry myself. Never wanting to be a burden, not always one-hundred-percent comfortable with someone intensely watching my body unless we were in the throes of something.

But there was something about this moment, this man, that look in his eyes that had me sliding my arms through the holes of the top, allowing him to pull the wet material forward, dropping it down to my side, his gaze on mine for a long moment before dipping, moving over my breasts, my nipples twisted tight from cold and more than a little desire.

A deep breath inflated Trip's chest as his hands rose, running the towel over my breasts, wiping away all water.

His thumb grazed my nipple, an unexpected touch that had my breath catching, his air exhaling.

He didn't linger, though, reaching to grab the blanket, yanking it away from my body completely, the towel lifting again to rub across my bare belly, over the tops of my thighs, down my calves, the tops of my feet.

"Stand up, babe," he demanded, gaze scorching into mine.

There was no hesitation.

I rose up to my feet, towering over him.

His hands slid up my thighs, snagging the wet material of my bathing suit bottom, slowly sliding it down.

It was right as my suit slipped down my thighs to pool at my feet that I realized how perfect our positions were, how he had clearly planned this.

Even as the realization was settling in, his hand was snagging my knee, pulling it wider, settling it up on the ledge of the fireplace, his face sliding between, tracing up my cleft, lavishing over my clit.

Pleasure was a hot, nearly painful thing, sapping all the strength from my thighs, making me bend forward to place my hands down on his shoulders as my breathing shallowed out, as my gasps became whimpers that quickly turned into moans.

Only then, as my thighs began to shake, did he pull away, get to his feet, guide me toward the bed, covering my body with his own.

My legs spread, inviting him between.

His towel slipped away, his cock sliding against my slick cleft, head rubbing over my clit.

THERE BETTER BE PIE

His lips sealed over mine, hard, demanding, bringing the need to a fever pitch, my hips grinding up against him, nails raking down his back.

His body shifted to the side, arm going out to the nightstand where my purse was situated, fumbling for a moment before coming back with the foil, protecting us as my lips moved down his neck, the stubble burning down my cheek.

Trip's arms planted, his upper body pushing up, allowing him to look down at me, watch me for a long moment as my hips shifted shamelessly against his, begging for release.

"Trip, please," I begged, hips lifting once again.

This time, though, he slid deep inside, taking every inch of me, his eyes closing as he sucked in a deep breath when my muscles tensed around him, as my hips moved in quick, desperate circles.

Control snapped, his eyes opened as he slid out of me, then slammed back in.

Deep.
Hard.
Deliberate.
Perfect.

My nails raked across his shoulders as his body claimed mine, as my hips rose to meet his need, demanding more, demanding everything. Something I was all too happy to give to him.

"Come, Princess," he demanded, hips grinding into mine, cock thrusting—faster, more desperate.

As if I had been waiting for permission, the orgasm slammed through my body—an intense white heat that started at the base of my spine and exploded outward, overtaking me completely, dragging him with me, slamming deep, hissing out my name as he came.

Bodies spent, we stayed there for several long moments, trying to bring some order back to the chaos formerly known as our bodies, breathing hard, heartbeats pounding, sweat drying.

Drained, yes.

But also happy.

Floating.

My body might have been spent, but my mind, my mind had never been more clear.

All those years of battling.

We could have been doing this instead.

In the future, I planned to make the correct decision.

Over and over and over.

Until our bodies just couldn't take it anymore.

"Thought you couldn't get hotter than when you were screaming at me," Trip said a long moment later, rolling off to my side, hand sliding down my belly. "I was wrong."

"Wait," I said, eyes getting small. "You *liked* arguing with me?"

"I loved arguing with you," he clarified. "Couldn't get enough of it."

Maybe I normally would have been mad at him for that. Before. Before I understood. How thin—almost nonexistent—that line between hate and love actually was.

Not that I loved Trip.

Not yet.

But for the first time, I didn't think it was the most absurd thing I had ever heard before.

"I think—in the future—anytime you want to argue with me, I propose we do this instead."

"Think I can live with that compromise," he said, smile warm, eyes gooey.

With that, he rolled off the other side of the bed, disappearing into the bathroom for a moment before coming back out, gloriously naked.

"What?" I asked when he stood there at the end of the bed.

"Is there any pie left?" he asked, making my smile break out.

I had a feeling there would always, always be pie.

"Let's go see."

CHAPTER TWELVE

Trip

We spent the next two days almost always naked. In her bed. In my bed. On the couch. In the hot tub. Over the kitchen island while she was getting ready to roll out dough to make another pie, leaving us both almost completely covered in flour afterward, sharing a shower, sharing our bodies, then sharing that pie when we eventually got it finished.

The real world would come back soon enough; I found myself in no rush to get back to it, enjoying our little oasis more than I could have ever realized.

The morning following finally giving into each other, into the passion that had always been there from the very beginning, buried under much more convenient hatred, Kathy finally called.

She confessed almost instantly, the words tumbling out, loud enough for me to hear even standing several feet away from Jett.

Actually, it was your father's idea.
I had a hard time picturing that.

THERE BETTER BE PIE

But, then again, had you never seen Mitch around his wife, you never would have imagined him to be the romantic he truly was.

Maybe the right woman just brought that out of you.

And maybe Mitch and Kathy had always been able to see what we had been desperately trying not to. Just how compatible we really were. How good we could be if we managed to get our heads out of our asses and admitted that all our disagreements were based on a core misunderstanding about our roles in Mitch's life.

Now that it was all out on the table, it was hard to believe we'd spent years sniping and snapping and dreading running into each other, criticizing every little thing because, well, it was impossible to find any *big* things about each other that we hated.

Animosity gone, Jett was every bit the Sunshine people so often referred to her as. She was deeply passionate about even the smallest things—movies, TV, music, what flavors did and did not go together—and intensely loyal to those that mattered most to her. She cared about the environment and animals and had a long-held wish to have a pet pig someday that stemmed from an obsession with *Charlotte's Web* as a kid.

She sang—horribly—when she was happy.

She answered the phone like each call was the first time she'd heard someone's voice in a decade.

She beamed at me when I walked in a room.

She reached for my hand in her sleep.

She made food for me and watched me with eager eyes when I dug in, like she enjoyed nourishing me, like she enjoyed *my* enjoyment.

It was everything I had never realized I wanted.

And I never wanted to let it go now that I found it, now that it belonged to me.

"What happens now?" Jett asked, gaze out the front windows toward the cleared driveway, watching the snow plow do one final lap down the road leading toward it.

There were no more excuses.

It was time to go back to our lives.

"Depends on how stubborn you are going to choose to be."

"What is that supposed to mean?" she asked, shooting small eyes at me.

"Careful," I said, smirking. "As per our agreement, if you keep that attitude up, we're going to be putting on one hell of a show for the staff when they come by." Which we were forewarned they would be as soon as the road was cleared, to come in and help us clean, clear out the food, get the house ready for no one to be there for another whole year.

To that, her lips curved up into a smile. "No attitude. I just don't know what you think I am being stubborn about."

"Nothing yet, but I have a feeling that it is coming."

"About what happens next," I clarified. "If you are going to go along with what we both know is going to be your future sooner or later, or if you are going to dig your heels in, be a pain in the ass, and insist it *has* to be later."

"And just how am I going to go about being a pain in the ass in this situation?"

"By insisting you have to go back to the city, go back to your job, go back to your life—"

"But I *do* have to go back to the city, back to my job, back to my life. Just like you have to go back to yours."

"Look, we both know what is going to happen eventually. You are going to quit that job. You are going to move back to Pennsylvania, buy that house you want, come back to Kensley. There is no question that you see that as your future now, right?"

"Right," she agreed, nodding.

"So you know you want that. You know you can have that. The stubbornness would be you insisting that needs to happen one—or five—years down the road."

"I guess you have a point," she agreed, glancing down at her phone, one that had been dinging pretty incessantly since we had woken up. She was, technically, back on the clock, even if she was working remotely.

"Go back to the city. Get your shit in order. Give your notice. Then come to Pennsylvania."

"You make it sound so easy."

"Because it is easy, Princess. You just have to make those choices."

Her gaze fell, thinking it through, being someone who needed to process things for a minute before she could really wrap her head around it.

"I guess I could move back in with my parents for a while so I can job hunt."

"No."

"What do you mean no? They'd be happy to have me."

"Yeah, well, I think I would be happier to have you," I told her.

I hadn't even thought that offer through. But even with it out there, I realized I didn't want to take it back.

I did want her there with me.

I wanted more of this.

I wanted all of this that I could get.

"You just want me to be there to make you more pie."

"Well, yeah, there is that," I agreed, moving over toward her, wrapping my arms around her lower back, looking down at her. "Say yes," I demanded.

There was a hesitation.

Of about three seconds.

"Yes."

I was going to get her.

And all the pie I could eat.

It sounded pretty freaking perfect to me.

EPILOGUE

Juliette - One Year Later

"You're quiet," my mother said, eyes a little concerned as she brushed her hair out of her face, reaching for the canister of the flour to start rolling out the dough for her pecan pie.

"Am I?" I asked, shaking my head, having trouble adjusting to my newfound tiredness. Without the aid of coffee. "I'm a little worn out," I admitted.

Four a.m. seemed to come earlier this year than any before. And it had nothing to do with how I'd slept the night before. Which had been like the dead. But no matter how much sleep I got, my body wanted more more more. Despite how little I did. The day before, the extent of my exertion was sitting in the passenger seat watching the world go by me, then planting myself on the couch watching TV with my dad.

"Go back upstairs, curl up with your man," she suggested, smile sweet. "I have this."

"No no. I wait all year for this," I assured her. It was the truth. It didn't matter that we now lived in the same town, that I saw her every Sunday in my halfway remodeled kitchen, eating off the tile backsplash samples I seemed incapable of choosing between as makeshift placemats.

That was our everyday thing.

This?

This was our Thanksgiving thing.

My favorite holiday.

All of our favorite.

Maybe even more so now.

It was the one holiday we all spent together. It was when my mother and I went over-the-top to make a memorable meal. It was when we stopped to reflect on things we were grateful for.

And now, well, it was the anniversary of Trip and I finally realizing something my mother and father had known nearly all along. That we were supposed to be together. Just like they were. Sure, they were willing to let us go through the motions much like they had needed to, deal with the ups and downs, find out the truth for ourselves in our own time, but they had been rooting for us almost all along.

I didn't want to ruin the day just because it seemed like there was a weight constantly pressing down on my eyelids, begging them to close for just another couple minutes.

"Yes, Pudge, honey, but this is the first year you are having to prepare Thanksgiving while *pregnant*, so some exceptions must be made."

My hand immediately slapped down on my stomach, one I was pretty sure looked just as it always had still.

"How did you know?"

"Just like you, Jetty, I was practically narcoleptic my first trimester. You've been dragging for a few weeks now. I keep waiting for the announcement. But..."

"I didn't tell Trip yet," I told her.

"What? Why not? This is happy news!"

"It is," I agreed, nodding. Trip wanted kids. I wanted kids. We'd just never agreed on a timeline for that.

THERE BETTER BE PIE

And I had just wanted to be sure first. Then felt a little unsure how to tell him. "I kind of decided that waiting and telling him here would be kind of sweet."

"Not kind of sweet," she corrected. "Very sweet."

"What's very sweet?" Trip asked, moving past me to get a coffee, brows furrowing when I shook my head, despite stifling a yawn.

"Apple pie," I told him, changing the topic.

"Which brings me to why I am up at this hour," he said, twisting the top onto a travel mug of coffee. "I need to go for a run to build up my appetite for later," he told me, smile genuine.

He'd been talking about the Thanksgiving menu for weeks, been demanding I would once again make him Thanksgiving pierogi, that we would get back up after our turkey comas to watch *Home for the Holidays* again, that every tradition would stay just as they always had been.

"How about you come and meet me at the fire pit in half an hour? I won't keep you long. I know you have to bake. And we have a parade to watch. But just to have a couple quiet minutes."

"Okay. I'll meet you there," I agreed, leaning a bit into the kiss he pressed at my temple on his way past me.

"You know what? I think this might be the perfect opportunity for you to tell him, Pudge," my mom suggested.

And, well, she was right.

On that note, I got the filling made for my pie then rushed upstairs to get the box I had carefully tucked away with my shoes—a suitcase Trip would never go inside— then bundling up and making my way down the old familiar path, realizing this would likely be the last time I would do so alone, that the next year, I could have a little one doing it with me, someone else to share traditions with.

By the time I made it to the fire pit, my heart was so full it was near to bursting.

When I saw Trip there building up the fire, it simply overflowed.

THERE BETTER BE PIE

"There you are," he said, smiling as he dropped down on one of the stone seats, patting the one next to him. "What do you have there?" he asked, nodding toward the box I was awkwardly cradling between both hands in my lap.

"A present," I told him, stomach fluttering around.

"For me?"

"Yeah."

"Can I have it?" he asked, smirking when I kept gripping it like a life vest.

"I, ah, yeah. Here," I said, practically throwing it at him, making his brows furrow as he reached for the lid, slowly pulling it open, then parting the tissue paper to reveal the pair of plain white baby shoes.

"Princess," he said, voice a little thick. "I thought you said you were bad at giving presents," he told me, gaze lifting, eyes filled with all the love and excitement I was feeling.

"You're happy?" I asked, already seeing the answer in his face. A face I had come to love more than I could say over the past year. Even when we were getting dangerously close to yelling at each other just a month and a half before over what kind of crown molding to use in the house we were working on. Before remembering our agreement about fights. And breaking in the dining room table. And, I suspected, creating the life currently growing inside me.

"Yes. And no," he said, making my stomach drop.

"No?" I asked.

"Yeah, 'cause, well, you kind of upstaged me," he told me, making my brows furrowing.

"Upstaged you?" I repeated.

"Yeah. Now asking you to marry me isn't going to be nearly as epic," he said, reaching into his pocket to produce the ring.

It was, though.

Epic.

"Trip..."

THERE BETTER BE PIE

"Marry me," he demanded, already slipping the ring onto my finger. "I want to build a lifetime of traditions with you," he added, closing his hand over mine, giving it a squeeze.

"You just want a lifetime of pie," I told him, feeling a tear slide down my cheek.

"Well, yeah," he agreed, smiling huge. "There better be pie."

XX

ALSO BY JESSICA GADZIALA

If you liked this book, check out these other series and titles in the NAVESINK BANK UNIVERSE:

The Henchmen MC
Reign
Cash
Wolf
Repo
Duke
Renny
Lazarus
Pagan
Cyrus
Edison
Reeve
Sugar
The Fall of V
Adler
Roderick
Virgin
Roan
Camden

The Savages
Monster
Killer
Savior

Mallick Brothers
For A Good Time, Call
Shane
Ryan
Mark
Eli
Charlie & Helen: Back to the Beginning

Investigators
367 Days
14 Weeks
4 Months

Dark
Dark Mysteries
Dark Secrets
Dark Horse

Professionals
The Fixer
The Ghost
The Messenger
The General
The Babysitter
The Middle Man

Rivers Brothers
Lift You Up

STANDALONES WITHIN NAVESINK BANK:
Vigilante
Grudge Match

OTHER SERIES AND STANDALONES:

Stars Landing
What The Heart Needs
What The Heart Wants
What The Heart Finds
What The Heart Knows
The Stars Landing Deviant
What The Heart Learns

Surrogate
The Sex Surrogate
Dr. Chase Hudson

The Green Series
Into the Green
Escape from the Green

DEBT
Dissent
Stuffed: A Thanksgiving Romance
Unwrapped
Peace, Love, & Macarons
A Navesink Bank Christmas
Don't Come
Fix It Up
N.Y.E.
faire l'amour
Revenge

ABOUT THE AUTHOR

Jessica Gadziala is a full-time writer, parrot enthusiast, and coffee drinker from New Jersey. She enjoys short rides to the book store, sad songs, and cold weather.

She is very active on Goodreads, Facebook, as well as her personal groups on those sites. Join in. She's friendly.

STALK HER!

Connect with Jessica:

Facebook: https://www.facebook.com/JessicaGadziala/
Facebook Group: https://www.facebook.com/groups/314540025563403/

Goodreads: https://www.goodreads.com/author/show/13800950.Jessica_Gadziala
Goodreads Group: https://www.goodreads.com/group/show/177944-jessica-gadziala-books-and-bullsh

Twitter: @JessicaGadziala

JessicaGadziala.com

<3/ Jessica

Made in the USA
Monee, IL
08 November 2024